Henry Mazyck Clarkson

Songs of Love and War

Henry Mazyck Clarkson

Songs of Love and War

ISBN/EAN: 9783337265595

Printed in Europe, USA, Canada, Australia, Japan

Cover: Foto ©Andreas Hilbeck / pixelio.de

More available books at **www.hansebooks.com**

SONGS

OF

LOVE AND WAR

BY

HENRY MAZYCK CLARKSON, A. M., M. D.

MANASSAS JOURNAL PRESS
MANASSAS, VA.
1898

TO MY WIFE

AND CHILDREN,

WHOSE CONSTANT LOVE AND LOYALTY

HAVE CHIEFLY INSPIRED THEM,

I AFFECTIONATEY DEDICATE

THESE PAGES.

CONTENTS:

POLITICAL.

WAR.

SONGS OF LOVE AND WAR.

To W. H. W. MORAN, Esq.

You wonder, my friend, why so seldom I print
  The fanciful thoughts which I weave into
    verse;
You flatter my Muse by your delicate hint
  Of fame in the future, of gold in my purse:
You ask why I write, if but few are to read;
  You talk of the wasting of talent and time;
I covet not fame, am accustomed to need,
  And men do not offer their riches for rhyme.

Consider the lark! How he rises on wing,
  And mounts to the sky through ethereal air!
He sings as he soars; 'tis his nature to sing,
  To warble his notes though no listener be
    near:
I seek not for fortune, I sigh not for fame,
  I follow my Muse into forest, or street;
In sorrow, in gladness, I sing all the same,
  I sing because singing itself is so sweet.

Wateree, Va., Oct. 22, 1897.

DO YOU REMEMBER?

Do you remember, Jean, that summer evening,
    long ago,
      In mild July,
When by Rivanna's banks we strolled, mean-
    dering with its flow—
      Just you and I?
Oh, I recall the very dress you wore!   No fairy
    sight
      Could fairer seem,
As in your chaste and simple white, you walked,
    a vision bright
      As poet's dream!

And I remember 'round your throat a bit of
    ancient lace,
      And from your pin
A ribbon fluttering with delight, whene'er it
    touched your face,
      Or dimpled chin;
Another clasped your pretty waist, and both
    were dainty blue,
      Just like your eyes—
That is—if anything God ever made could
    match that hue,
      Except the skies.

And when I watched the evening star rise in
    the rosy west
      And look at you,
I thought it flushed to see the gem that glit-
    tered on your breast,

And jealous grew,
And once or twice, by dint of chance, I saw
two slippers peep,
Too shy to stay,
And though I caught your coy, your conscious
glance, I could not keep
My eyes away!

For I was very deep in love—in love with eyes
of blue,
And faultless feet—
It might have been with mind or heart, I only
knew that you
Were very sweet;
So sweet the birds would cease their evening
songs to see you pass,
Ere seeking rest,
And I—I would have gladly stooped to kiss the
bending grass
Your feet had pressed.

Long years have passed since then, my Jean,
full freighted with the bliss
Of wedded life—
'Twas on that very day you promised me, with
virgin kiss,
To be my wife;
And when I sought one more caress, you said,
with tempting smile,
"Nay, Love, no more;"
But I was very deep in love, and in true lover's
style,
I stole a score.

E'en now I languish for your kiss, for you are
    very sweet,
        And could I know
That nevermore with mine those warm respon-
    sive lips would meet,
        In weal or woe,
I'd find again those flowery banks, where soft
    Rivanna's wave
        Still friendly flows,
And 'neath those silent waters seek a kind for-
    getful grave
        For love's repose.

Old Point Comfort, Va.

TO A LEAF UNDER A BROOCH.

Ah! little leaf, how covet I
    Your comfortable rest!
How cosily you seem to lie
    Upon my lady's breast!
And though I know 'tis vain to sigh
    To be, like thee, caressed;
Yet, ah! how happy I could die
    To be so blessed.

I would I were her favorite flower,
    Nor sunned by summer sky,
But growing in her chosen bower,
    Beneath her azure eye:
How eagerly I'd lift my head
    To meet her maiden kiss;

To make, perchance, her breast my bed,
  A bed of bliss!

Now nestling on her neck, the while
  I'd list to thought within,
Then, basking in her sunny smile,
  I'd touch her dimpled chin:
From damask cheek and ruby lip
  I'd steel a roseate hue;
Her eyes, my skies, from them I'd sip
  My only dew.

What though I perish in my bliss,
  So I but hear her sigh!
What pleasure half so sweet as this—
  Upon her breast to die!
Her warm young bosom be my bier,
  My dirge, her lulling breath;
In love, I still would linger there,
  Yes, e'en in death.

WHAT THE ANGEL BROUGHT US.

In the early days of autumn,
  In the bright autumnal days,
When the Indian-summer sunlight
  Slants its soft September rays,
In my chamber I lay dreaming
  Of a sick one dear to me,
Of her young maternal yearnings
  For a life that was to be.

By her bed-side I was dreaming
  In the curtained light of day,
Till the purpling of the morning
  Brightened into streaks of gray—
I was dreaming that an angel,
  Hovering o'er the loved one's couch,
Fanned her with a breath of Heaven,
  Healed her with his holy touch—

Seeming, too, to carry something,
  Something sheltered 'neath his wing;
Then he laid it down, and left it,
  Left the wee but wondrous thing,
And he scarcely pressed the carpet,
  Passing by me where I lay—
Touched me with his wing as lightly,
  As an aspen-leaf at play.

But that gentle touch awoke me,
  And the rosy flush of dawn,
Falling on the lovely sufferer,
  Showed the angel-form was gone;

But I saw the angel's burden
   Tightly to her bosom pressed—
Baby fingers as she slumbered,
   Toying with her marble breast.

And I kissed the dainty fingers,
   When two lips so sweetly smiled,
Could I tell which was the sweetest—
   Mother pale—or dimpled child?
But I know, no angel ever
   Sweeter boon or blessing bore,
And no father and no mother
   Welcomed such a babe before.

For her face is like the morning,
   Like the morning-star, her eye,
And her hair is like the sun-light
   Of the Indian-summer sky.
Such the gift the angel brought us—
   Baby with her winsome ways—
In the early days of autumn,
   In the bright autumnal days.

THE DEATH OF THE MAIDEN.

Through a forest sere and sober,
In the golden-clad October,
Autumn winds were softly sighing,
Summer leaflets falling, flying,
    Lying, dying everywhere.
We were wandering, slowly walking,
I was wooing, lowly talking,
Ah! it seems so very lately,
With a maiden tall and stately,
    With a maiden frail and fair.

How she lingered as she listened!
And her eyes with tear-drops glistened,
All her brow and bosom blushing,
Came her words so gently gushing—
    "Take me—love me—I am thine."
Oh! those words were whispered lowly!
And her vow it seemed so holy,
As a vesper psalm so saintly,
Falling sweetly, falling faintly,
    As a psalmody divine!

Sweet those moments of our meeting!
Sweet, though few and far too fleeting!
Halcyon hours of happy dreaming,
All of life with beauty teeming
    In those gladsome, golden hours!
Blissful were the thoughts we pondered,
Peaceful all the ways we wandered,
Through the woods and meadows mellow,
Through the waving fields of yellow,
    Through the sunny autumn flowers!

Came then sickness, and in anguish,
Day by day, we watched her languish,
Watched her waning, watched her wasting,
Oh! the agony of tasting
    Those mad moments of despair!
Vain was all the art of healing,
Blight was o'er her beauty stealing,
Vain our wailing, vain our weeping,
Cruel death came creeping, creeping,
    Caring not that she was fair.

After one long night of sorrow,
Ere the dawning of the morrow,
From the tapers dimly burning,
Softly to the maiden turning,
    Mourners whispered, "she is dead!"
Doubting, fearing, still uncertain,
Dreading yet to lift the curtain,
Something seemed to hover 'round her;
Angels, then I knew had found her—
    Knew I then her soul had fled.

From her lifeless form they tore me,
From her cold embrace they bore me,
But our souls they could not sever,
We shall meet again forever,
    Aye, forever, hand in hand.
Time is flowing, time is flowing,
On her grave the grass is growing,
Waves the willow o'er her weeping,
But her sainted soul is sleeping,
    Waiting in the spirit-land.

MY SWEETHEART IS COMING THEN.

Hear the blue-birds, how they warble,
  Chant and chirrup in the air!
Why, old Winter, do you linger?
  Longer days will soon be here;
Soon the sun will shine more brightly,
  And my heart be glad again,
Then these arms will welcome some one—
  My sweetheart is coming then.

Hear the lark, too! Do you wonder
  That my heart should want to sing?
Old friend, do you grieve to see me
  Kiss my hand to coming Spring?
In the birth-days of the daisies,
  When the snow-drops clothe the glen,
Some one sweeter than the snow-drops—
  My sweetheart is coming then.

In the eventide of Easter,
  When the moonlight lingers late,
And the mocking-bird is singing
  Nightly to his wistful mate—
In the Easter-month of lovers,
  When the moon is full again,
Some one, who can sing as sweetly—
  My sweetheart is coming then.

Old friend, do you wonder at me,
  Wonder I should want to sing,
When all nature wakes to greet the
  Footsteps that will come in Spring?

Farewell! you've been kind, old Winter;
Maybe when you come again,
Both of us will bid you welcome—
My sweetheart will be mine then.

March 25th.

YOUNG JENNIE LANIER.

Oh! hear ye the fall of light feet in the hall?
'Tis the sound of the step of a maiden fair.
The carpet how blessed, by those dainty feet
     pressed!
          So proud to be laden
          With such a dear maiden!
As falls the white flake of light snow on the
     lake,
So falls the soft step of young Jennie Lanier.

My fond heart rejoice, for I hear her sweet voice,
     Like the warble of birds on the balmy air;
It rises and swells like the rhythm of bells,
          Its melody fills me,
          With happiness thrills me;
Like music in dreams, like a lullaby seems
     The sound of the voice of sweet Jennie Lanier.

No star in the sky is as bright as her eye,
     And the sun cannot vie with her golden hair,
And let her but speak, see o'er bosom and cheek
          The crimson blood rushes,
          And mounts into blushes!

No bloom can eclipse her soft roseate lips,
  The rosy red lips of fair Jennie Lanier.

I yearn and I pine for her heart to be mine,
  Just to live in her life would be happiness
    rare,
I would barter a throne just to call her my own;
      And yet she is cruel,
      This choice little jewel;
I never have met such a cruel coquette,
  So coy a coquette as sly Jennie Lanier.

Tho' prudish, tho' proud, when we meet in a
    crowd,
  With her pretty head held so high in the air,
She passes not by, if none others are nigh,
      But graciously greets me
      With smiles when she meets me:
Yet who could e'er be half so precious to me,
  As Jennie, bewitching young Jennie Lanier!

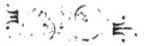

MAD.

The pale-faced moon, in a fleecy cloud,
    Looks cold and blank from her curtained bed,
Like a visage veiled in a snowy shroud—
    The stiff, stark face of a woman dead.
Avaunt, pale vision! Out, out from the skies;
    I know whose face is reflected there—
That woman's face with its dead, dull eyes,
    That chills my veins with its vacant stare.

Just so she looked, when they laid her down,
    With marks of blood on her face and feet;
With tell-tale stains on her tattered gown;
    Just so she lay in her winding sheet;
Just so she seemed in a cloud to float,
    While my senses reeled and my sight grew
        dim,
With murder marks on her pearly throat;
    Just so she paled as a spectre grim.

'Twas years ago, on a shadowy night,
    One Christmas-eve of the long ago,
The moon looked down with a lurid light
    On the wild and wintry world below—
With baleful beams, through an open glade,
    Peered mournfully down at Maud and me,
As we silent paused in the solemn shade,
    In the fitful shade of a sombre tree.

The night seemed weird, as the dead leaves
        stirred
    Over our heads in the hoary tree,

Whilst never a word, not a whispered word
   Was spoken at all by Maud or me;   •
For my brain was crazed by the demon, Wine;
   My body was reeling to and fro,
While the moon turned pale, ashamed to shine
   On the sorrowful scene of sin below.

As we stood in silence, side by side,
   In the dismal shade of the dusky tree,
In the gloomy haze of the night's noon-tide,
   How beautiful seemed my Maud to me!
But the damning bowl my brain had crazed;
   My blood beat fast with its subtile flow;
And the moon alone saw my arm upraised,
   Only the moon saw the fatal blow.

   *   *   *   *   *   *   *   *

How gracefully lay my Maud at rest,
   Her beautiful raven hair afloat,
With gems of blood on her jewelled breast,
   With beads of blood on her pearly throat;
Ah! I loved my lovely Maud that night,
   As the moon fell full on her upturned face
And wanton winds, o'er her bosom white,
   Were lightly lifting the envied lace!

We slept, both slept till the Christmas dawn,
   Dreaming our dreams till the break of day;
I dreamed that my beautiful Maud was gone,
   Gone with the beams of the moon away.
I awoke—and my hands were fast in chains
   And felon fetters were around my feet,
Whilst Maud, all marred by murder stains,
   Lay stiff and stark in a winding sheet.

I watched my Maud in her flowing shroud,
　I watched till my weeping eyes were dim,
Till she seemed to float on a fleecy cloud,
　Paling away as a spectre grim;
And I see her yet beyond the stars,
　I watch her form in the midnight skies;
I see her face through my prison bars—
　That woman's face with its dead dull eyes.

They call me mad, and with felon chains
　They bind me fast to my prison floor,
Where I nightly hear the mournful strains
　Of the winter winds in their wild uproar;
Where naught I hear but my clanking chains
　And the howling winds at my dungeon door,
Where naught I see but the mocking stains
　Of that face in the moon forevermore.

Avaunt, pale moon, with your ghostly glare!
　Look not so mournfully on me below;
You freeze my heart with a frenzied fear;
　You fill my soul with a fearful woe;
You drive me mad when I see you shine;
　Avaunt from the sky with your goblin glow!
You know 'twas the deed of the demon Wine—
　'Twas the demon Wine, that dealt the blow!

THE FORGET-ME-NOTS.

TO MARGUERITE.

The roses in my garden may proudly bloom
    and blow,
The graceful oleanders in stateliness may grow,
Camellias may adorn the coquettish beauty's
    head,
And orange blossoms deck her, who is waiting
    to be wed;
The lily, and the laurel which wreathes the
    brow of fame—
'Tis all God's handiwork, under whatsoever
    name—
But the sweetest flowers of all, the sweetest
    that I ken,
Are the blue Forget-me-nots, which hide from
    haunts of men—
The fairest things, which blossom in garden or
    in glen—
Yellow-eyed Forget-me-nots, which skirt the
    open fen.
Little shy Forget-me-nots, which shun the gaze
    of men.

The princess in her palace, the proudly born
    and bred,
The heiress condescending to bow her haughty
    head,
The beauty 'neath the lights, pirouetting in
    the dance,
The sly coquette who throws all her cunning
    in her glance,

Aspasias and Delilahs may ply their artful
   wiles—
They all may lavish on me the blandest of their
   smiles—
But sweetest of them all in the castle, or the cot,
The little maiden, who, like the meek Forget-
   me-not,
Adorning any station which happens to her
   lot—
Looks up with modest greeting from some
   neglected spot—
Looks up between her blushes, to plead "forget
   me not."

I BELIEVE.

Some day, some one will come and close these
   eyes,
   And say, "God's will be done—'tis better so,"
And sad "Amens" from quivering lips will rise,
   But one poor heart will cry, crushed down
      by woe,
   "Alas! Alas! He loved—he loved me so!"

Ay! loved thee so, that tho' these lips be dumb,
   Yet, when that plaint shall reach the spirit-
      sphere,
I do believe this spirit back will come,
   And in the drapery of dreams draw near
   The only being which it worshipped here.

Ay, worshipped here, but I will tell thee then,
  In thrilling tones of joy not known before—
A Home for us, not made by hands of men—
  Beyond the shadowy vale, a shining shore,
  Where you and I can rest forevermore!

Sweet Sabbath to our souls! Ear hath not heard
  A kinder welcome than such message bears!
Ah! Rest, sweet Rest! What rapture in the
    word!
  Sweet rest to those who toil, and reap but
    tares—
  Poor feet worn weary with the work of years.

Beloved: I believe, that when these eyes,
  From death's sweet calm to newer scenes
    shall wake,
And, in the spirit, I shall walk the skies—
  That, earthward oft, this soul its flight will
    take,
  And talk with thee, in dreams, for Love's
    sweet sake.

And I believe, that Love, grown strong in life,
  Is stronger yet in death—and tho' the cross
Be hard—yet, Death, the conquerer in the strife,
  In pity, strips poor Love of earthly dross,
  And Love grows stronger, holier for the loss.

UNDER THE ORCHARD TREE.

Above us was bending the blue of the skies,
Together we stood in the shade of the tree;
More blue than the skies shone her beautiful
eyes,
More bright was her face than the morning
to me.
All ruddy and ripe hung the fruit overhead,
As luscious and tempting as fruit ever grew;
More tempting to me was the roseate red
Of cheeks, and of lips the most luscious I
knew.

The orchard seemed sweet as an Eden could be,
The Eve of my Eden looked faultlessly fair;
Could Adam have seen us, my charmer and me,
I think he would have envied me dallying
there.
I wonder if Satan was walking that day!
He might have been coiled in the tall orchard
grass;
He lured me to stay in his old subtle way—
He looked through the languishing eyes of
the lass.

He came in the guise of young Cupid, I know,
The little god's image I saw in her eye;
I winced, as I noted him bending his bow,
And winging each shaft with the breath of a
sigh.
I own 'tis imprudent to tell it in song;
I own 'twas not practicing proper restraint—

·I kissed her—just once! Yes, I know it was
   wrong,
  But lips such as hers would have tempted a
   saint.

HER GLOVE.

Only a little brown kid glove,
  With tiny, half-worn fingers,
And yet, it wakes a world of love,
  As thought around it lingers:
It brings to mind an absent hand,
  The tales of love told o'er it—
To me, the dearest in the land,
  The wee white hand that wore it.

And since this little hand I own,
  I hold no prize above it,
Nor would I give it for a throne,
  No other wealth I covet.
And so, I kiss my brown kid glove,
  And keep it as a token—
A pledge of all her plighted love,
  Of troth between us spoken.

Fisherman's Island, Va.

MY GOOD ANGEL.

Bright dawned the day when she was born,
  And softly smiled the summer weather;
A rarer perfume filled the morn,
  And all the song-birds sang together.

And now, a ministering angel—mixed
  With just a lump of human leaven—
She seems a mystic tie betwixt
  The sons of earth and saints of heaven,

With just enough of Eden's taint
  To light the spark of Eve within her—
Too much of earth to be a saint—
  Too much of heaven to be a sinner!

Nor would I have it otherwise,
  So sweet she is for being human—
Akin to angels of the skies,
  And yet I worship her as woman!

A WISH.

My soul, alas! has lost its song,
   Life has no solace left for me!
My Love, oh! linger not so long,
   Life is not life unshared with thee!
I yearn to see thee, face to face,
   To look deep down those eyes of thine,
Once more to feel thy fond embrace,
      That heart beat close to mine.

And like the favored bee, which sips
   The sweets the clover-blooms distil,
To find that these unhindered lips
   May kiss and kiss thine own, at will.
What Gilead bears such balm as this?
   What earthly Eden holds such charms?
To me—completeness of all bliss—
      The circle of thine arms!

Hampton Roads.

WHAT IS SHE LIKE?

"What is she like?" the neighbors ask,
    Dear wife, about our little Jean,
As if it were an easy task
    To liken her to aught I've seen—
        Our baby Jean.

As dainty as the daisies are,
    More graceful than the daffodils,
Her frisking feet make music far
    More sweet to me than merry rills
        Among the hills.

No romping air from out the South,
    At play among the flowers, but tries
To kiss her little rosy mouth,
    Enamored of the light that lies
        In her blue eyes.

And when I see the sunbeams chase
    Each other through her shining hair,
And watch the dimpling of her face,
    I wonder what I can compare
        With one so fair.

In truth, I find it hard to name
    A sweeter thing than Jean on earth;
But when I think of whom she came—
    Of her to whom she owes her birth,
        And all this worth,

'Tis then the neighbors hear me say,

She is your "second self."   'Tis true!
She grows more like you every day—
The sweetest thing I ever knew,
    Excepting you.

TO LUCY, WITH A PAIR OF GULL WINGS.

I send you, Sweet, the only things
    You further need to wear;
'Twas all you lacked—a pair of wings—
    To be an angel fair.

I merely ask, that in the flights
    Your spirit makes through space,
I'll hear you hovering by o'nights,
    And see you face to face.

Fisherman's Island, Va.

SHE DIED TO-DAY.

Telegram—Feb. 1, 1885.

From Fatherland, far, far away,
The message comes, "She died to-day;"
They little know what 'tis to see
Those sad, sad words they send to me.

They little know, that when she died,
My soul was hovering by her side,
The last to linger 'round her bier,
The saddest mourner weeping there.

They little know, that whilst I knelt
In spirit there, the thoughts I felt
Were thoughts, that would unbidden flow,
About the days long, long ago;

About one evening, most of all,
When in the old ancestral hall
We met—'twas when we both were young,
And love was all the song we sung.

I seemed to see her as she stood,
In the full flush of womanhood,
That night, beneath the chandelier,
With radiant eyes, and raven hair.

And then, I saw her as a bride,
Another standing by her side;
For fate had forced us far apart,
And I had lost her hand and heart.

Again I saw, as spirit sees,
A matron glad, and 'round her knees
Were pretty children at their play,
Brightening her thoughts through all the day.

Then on her bier, a woman fair,
With roses tangled in her hair,
I saw as plain, as plain could be,
And fair as love could paint for me.

Ye dull, dull dotards, who deny
That love has wings, ye know ye lie;
For though in body I was here,
My soul did see her on that bier.

Around her neck and pearly throat,
In rich dark folds, her hair afloat,
I saw her as she used to be,
The fairest thing on earth to me.

Again I see, as spirit sees—
I see her 'neath Celestial trees,
With harp in hand, and as she plays,
I catch a strain of vanished days.

Those days gone by! Alas! Alas!
Ah! well, God knows! So, let them pass;
But when from night's ethereal sphere
God hangs his starry chandelier,

Then with the music of the pines,
It seems, that heavenly harp combines,
As if a Seraph swept its strings,
To tune my thoughts to holier things.

'Tis then I see her far away,
And though they say, "she died to-day,"
Immortal halos crown her now,
And deathless beauty decks her brow.

THE NEW MOON.

I never see in the Western sky,
    When the weary day is ended,
A new moon lit like a lamp on high,
    Like a silver lamp suspended;
But I turn my steps some other way,
    And look leftward o'er my shoulder,
And wish for my loved one—wish and pray,
    That I to my heart might hold her.

Might fold my Love to my heart again,
    With a lover's kiss might greet her,
Might walk with her hand in mine, as when
    In the dusk I used to meet her;
But the moons they wax, the moons they wane,
    And to-night's new-moon is growing,
While I wish and wish—but wish in vain—
    The months with the moons are going!

Oh! crescent moon, shall I see her soon?
    Look down as you sail above her—
Does she wish for me to-night, oh moon,
    Or waits she some newer lover?
So like to a horse-shoe, hung up there,
    So like to a swinging sickle,

Your changing phases make me fear
  She, too, may be turning fickle.

Shine down, oh! moon, on her bosom shine,
  And tell me what you discover;
Is my Love quite true—her heart still mine,
  Or loves she a later lover?
Tell me, young moon, for I dreamed last night—
  What was it you found me dreaming?
      *   *   *   *   *
You lie, false moon!   Her soul is as white
  As the bright stars 'round you beaming!

Down, down from my sight, deceitful moon!
  I will not believe it!   Never!
I know these arms will enfold her soon—
  She vowed to be mine forever!
And the moons may wax, the moons may wane,
  And the new-moons all grow older,
I shall not wish for my Love in vain,
  But soon to my heart will hold her.

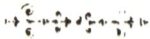

MY DAUGHTER.

Often 'mid the cares of business,
'Mid the bustle of the day,
Weary of my toilsome efforts,
Often do I turn away;
Turn away, and pause, and ponder
On a little maiden fair—
On a little girl, whose beauty
Meets me, greets me everywhere.

In the city, in the forest,
In the mansion, in the cot,
Nothing seems to make me happy,
Nothing smiles where she is not.
Dearest little fair thing is she,
Fairest, dearest that I know;
Like a memory, her laughter
Follows me where'er I go.

She has silken, shining tresses,
Cheeks of ever changing hue,
Languidly her long eye-lashes
Droop o'er dreamy depths of blue;
Golden sunlight seems to crown her,
Starlight flashing from her eye,
E'en the moonbeams fail to match her,
Paling, as she passes by.

Would you see this little maiden,
Would you know this peerless child?
Go with me to yonder cottage,
Humblest in the forest wild,

Humblest in its walls and rafters,
　Poorest in its floors and hearth;
Poor in these, and yet the proudest,
　Richest, rarest home on earth!

Go to yonder cottage with me,
　See, who greets me at the gate!
How she meets me with her kisses,
　Whether early, whether late!
See those young arms circled 'round me,
　Dimpling cheek pressed close to mine,
As the fragrant honeysuckle
　Throws its tendrils round the pine.

Then, no longer you will wonder,
　Why I hasten homeward so;
Why I linger in the gateway,
　Every morning loath to go.
Lover, clasp your dowered darling;
　Miser, count your shining gold;
But my peerless, blue-eyed daughter
　Is the dearest thing I hold.

Ellenwood, Va.

TO ELLEN, WITH A LOCK OF HAIR.

You ask, Ellen dear, for a lock of my hair,
To twine in a general family twist;
I send every thread I can possibly spare,
Whilst knowing each strand will be missed.

I hope 'twill suffice you—this one little lock—
Tho' surely you ask it, I think rather late,
For once I could boast quite a bountiful stock,
But now very bald is my pate.

Yes, once it was soft as the softest of down,
At least, by fair lips so I often was told;
They called it "a glossy, a beautiful brown,
Just touched with light tinges of gold."

But years, weary years have passed over my
head,
My Summer of life is fast slipping away;
Like leaves of the Autumn, turned ashy and
dead,
My locks now look sober and grey.

But what if old Winter's white draperies screen
The bare, leafless limbs of the storm-beaten
tree,
Within lies its great heart, yet living and green,
Nor broken, though shaken it be.

So I, too, while bending my head to the storm,
As time with its hoar-frosts has silvered it o'er,

Have kept my heart wakened, and vernal and
    warm,
  Not heeding the pitiless roar.

Ay, kept it alive, with its pulses in tune
  To. tender sweet thoughts of the loved and
    the true,
Thro' sunshine and tempest, at midnight and
    noon,
  Warmed up with affection for you.

So, take, my dear Sister, this lock which I send,
  In spite of the lustreless grey which you see,
And wreathe it with that of each kinsman and
    friend,
  As Love has long linked each to me.

MAGNUS M. LEWIS.

Dead, do they say ?   The good physician dead ?
A good man does not die.   He lays his head
A little while, "upon the lap of earth,"
Then waits serenely for the newer birth,
Which comes to him as comes the early dawn,
After the sweet and peaceful night is gone.
Ah! no, not dead!   The good man never dies;
But drops upon his couch with wistful eyes,
And with a farewell yearning look at those
He loves the best, he lets his eyelids close
In sleep—in dreamless sleep—but not for long,
For like the lark, that lifts his voice in song,
And mounts on light wings to the far off sky;
So soars and sings the good man's soul on high.
Then grieve not, widow; woman, do not weep,
Your God hath given your beloved sleep—
Sweet, restful sleep, and he shall wake to wear
The crown he won whilst walking with you here.
Ah! blissful sleep, from which the righteous rise!
Ah! blessed truth—the good man never dies!

THE THREAD OF GOLD.

A CONFESSION.

A single strand of sunny hair,
  Some blue-eyed blonde suggesting,
Lay curled upon my collar, where
  Her head had just been resting—
A tell-tale thread of yellow hair,
  Just where she had been leaning;
But Madam now has seen it there,
  And wants to know its meaning:—

"You know it is not mine," she said,
  "You need not, Sir, deny it,
That never grew upon this head;
  See, mine seems golden by it;
Yet oft you've vowed in other days,
  When youth and love were zealous,
When wont my hair and eyes to praise,
  You would not make me jealous."

"Judge not ungently, sweetest, best;
  In truth, I only told her,
When she was weary, just to rest
  Herself against my shoulder;
And when her head drooped on my arm,
  Oh, how could I resist her!
Her pretty mouth—well, what's the harm?
  Bewitched me, and—I kissed her!"

"You kissed her, too? What! more disgrace?
  And with the temptress tarried?

Enamored of a newer face,
  Forgot that you were married!
And did you—once, my king of men—
  More dainty charms discover?
Are other lips more tempting then,
  Than mine, my roving lover?"

"No, dearest, no! I know no bliss
  As sweet as your caresses;
So come and give me kiss for kiss,
  While your accused confesses:
This mischief-making thread of gold
  I own it—'tis another's—
A trophy from our three-year-old—
  How much 'tis like her mother's!

"So like to yours, I let it stay—
  You see, I'm still confessing—
Suggestive of that summer day,
  You waked to love's caressing;
And watching our sweet baby's lips,
  What mortal could resist her!
So like you to her finger-tips,
  What wonder that I kissed her!"

UNDER THE LEE.

Out on the veranda, under the lee
  I sat where the surf was kissing the sand,
And silence was settling down on the sea,
  And darkness was brooding over the land;
Not the dip of an oar disturbed the bay,
  No longer the feet of the waltzers stirred:
A sound as of footsteps coming my way—
  Two voices in whisper was all I heard.

Now nearer and nearer the walkers drew,
  And closer the sound of approaching feet,
Whilst clearer and clearer the voices grew,
  And one was strong, and the other was sweet;
The one soon dropped into a tender tone,
  The other was musical, soft and low;
The stronger was pleading "just one, my own,"
  The softer replied neither "yes," nor "no."

No answer I heard, but I caught a sound,
  I felt with the silence had come consent,
And my heart leaped up with a lighter bound,
  I knew what a kiss in the darkness meant;
And I hardly could stifle back a sigh,
  As I thought of a summer night of old—
Of a stolen kiss 'neath a starless sky—
  Of a time when a tender tale was told.

Hygeia Hotel.

THE REAPER RUTH.

TO L. S. G.

Aione, in a tangle of forest,
  In the slumberous afternoon,
I lay in the shadows inhaling
  The breath of the redolent June.
With many a quiver and caper,
  And chanting of lullabies sweet,
A brooklet came leaping and dancing,
  And rippling with joy at my feet.

And it seemed so buoyant and trusting,
  So close to its banks it would cling,
So full of its songs, and its laughter,
  So like unto a living thing,
I almost believed it would answer,
  Would I only bespeak it fair,
And tell me, just where it was going,
  And why it was murmuring there.

The melody of waters soothed me,
  That rhythmical voice of the stream,
And lulling my senses to languor,
  Induced me to sleep, and to dream;
And I saw what is seen but seldom,
  And only, when clothed in a dream—
I saw a most beautiful maiden
  Step forth from the tremulous stream.

She came, as came Eve into Eden,
  Nor seemed she afraid, or ashamed,

For virtue, the garment she stood in,
  Subdues e'en the tigers untamed—
So pure was the vestment that veiled her,
  So dazzling bright was her shield,
These eyes only saw in the creature
  Creation's perfection revealed.

She told me in musical numbers,
  And I know, that she told me truth—
That her errand was "never-ending,"
  That her name was "the Reaper Ruth—
And simple," she said, "is my mission,
  Distinctly ordained unto all—
To follow the mandates of duty,
  Wherever the message may call;

"To submit to commands with courage,
  And to go with a smiling face,
With sunshine about me, and singing—
  A sunbeam in the darkest place;
To help them who faint, or are fevered,
  To refreshen the famine-cursed,
To lift up the fallen or feeble,
  And to moisten the lips which thirst.

"For though we be lowly, or lofty,
  What gain, if we gather but leaves?
The Master, above us, is waiting
  To welcome us bringing in sheaves.
And such are the riches I'm reaping,
  These sheaves that I glean in my way,
And I know, the Head of the harvest
  Will count them on the harvest day."

Thus warbled the beautiful gleaner,
  Then vanished 'neath the purling stream,
And I thought of my toiling sisters,
  As I waked from my happy dream—
Then I knew who was Ruth, the Reaper,
  And that she sung a song of truth,
For the harvest is full of gleaners,
  And there's many a singing Ruth.

THAT DEAR OLD SWEET GUITAR:

Touch not that dear old sweet guitar,
  Wake not its silent strings,
Your sweetest music can but mar
  The memories it brings.
I've heard its notes 'neath starlit skies,
  Beside a cherished form,
Till soul met soul thro' love-lit eyes,
  And heart to heart beat warm.

Touch not that dear old sweet guitar,
  Your song but sadness stirs,
Better those chords be mute, by far,
  Than touched by hands not hers.
Those hands, which once did wake its tone,
  Have long since lain at rest—
Dear hands, which used to hold my own,
  Now clasped across her breast.

Touch not that dear old sweet guitar,
  Strike not one hallowed string,

You cannot know how sacred are
  The thoughts, which 'round it cling.
Those rusting chords, so dear to me,
  I cherish for her sake,
So let them, friend, still soundless be,
  Or, like my heart-strings, break.

A LESSON IN LACONICS.

One morning, when winding my way thro' the
    mountains,
  The storm had just ceased from its riotous
    orgies;
And rivulets, leaping from thousands of foun-
    tains,
  Were mingling in one, as they met in the
    gorges.
I own that both horse and her rider grew
    nervous,
  In view of our fording a freshet so rushing,
When in stepped a guide, just in good time to
    serve us,
  A maid of the mountains, bare-footed and
    blushing.

In stepped she as nimbly as naiad or fairy,
  So gracefully warding her skirts from the
    water,
Unconsciously posing, neat, picturesque Mary,
  The pride of the mountains, old Donaldson's
    daughter.

A piggin of butter she bore on her shoulder,
  From wading the current no suasion could
    keep her,
But cautiously stepping 'round ripple and
    ⌐boulder,
  She blushed a bit more as the waters grew
    deeper.

How pretty the toss of her tawny brown
    tresses!
  How comely the arm which she carried above
    her!
The curves of her lips, they seemed carved for
    caresses,
  The dew on them waiting for kiss of a lover!
Still anxious, I asked her, "How high is the
    water?"
And just to be civil, "the price of her butter,"
She answered, "Just up to my calves-and-a
    quarter,"
  Then went on her way, and naught else did
    she utter.

CUPID'S CATECHISM.

Is it sweet to love?
     Go ask the birds which sing
  Their dulcet measures to their mates in May;
Ask, if anything outside of Eden brings
  Such joy as making love in love's sweet way.

Is to be loved sweet?
     Go ask the blushing flower,
  Which droops because the enamored sun is
    missed,
If in her lofty lover's most ardent hour,
  She lifts not up her petals to be kissed.

And will sweet love last?
     Go ask the wooing sea,
  Whose waves forever kiss the willing shore—
Ask, if its encircling arms can sated be—
  The sea, that sick with kisses, sighs for more.

Is love's kiss so sweet?
     Go ask the bee, which drinks
  Its nectared dainties from elysian bowers,
If there be not perfume on the lips of pinks,
  Ambrosial sweetness in the cups of flowers.

And what makes love sweet?
     Go ask the arid waste,
  Which parches till the passing rain-cloud
    bursts,
What makes it so precious sweet a thing to taste
  The welcome drops for which its bosom
    thirsts.

Is love wedded sweet?
Go ask the oak, around
Whose form the fragrant honeysuckle clings,
If any truer joy 'neath Heaven is found,
Than mutual love to lives united brings.

WHO KNOWS?

Who knows but when that day of days has
come,
When God shall judge His children great and
small,
When you and I shall stand before Him dumb
With wonder at the justice done to all—

Who knows but you, my friend, whom fate
has blessed,
Whom fortune favors with its fondest smiles,
Who never felt the ceaseless, sad unrest,
Of tempted souls beset by Satan's wiles—

Who knows but we, accounted good by some,
Because our sins have not been seen of men—
Who knows but when that judgment-day shall
come,
That you and I will wonder mostly then,

To see that some, whom we call wicked here,
Have harps attuned to joy around God's
throne,
Whilst we ourselves no robes of welcome wear,

But stand condemned to reap as we have
  sown ?

God giveth strength to some—desires to all ;
  What strain that strength can bear He
    knoweth, too:
Judge not, my friend, lest judgment on you fall,
  Enough to know God giveth strength to you.

Stone not the fallen then, vain Pharisee,
  Nor wreck the soul already wrung by woes;
God makes allowances for you and me,
  And, maybe, for poor Magdalene.   Who
    knows ?

MEMORIES.

With the blooming of the daisies,
  When the birds begin to sing,
With the coming of the cowslips
  And the laughing of the Spring,
It is then that I remember,
  Oh! that I could hush these sighs,
Then it is that I am mindful
  What a matchless pair of eyes
Used to meet me in the meadow,
  When the birds began to sing,
With the blooming of the daisies,
  And the laughing of the Spring.

When the moonbeams on the leaflet

Leave their lines of silver light,
And the katydid keeps calling
    Through the silent summer night;
It is then I think it over—
    Would that I could not recall
How devotedly I loved her,
    How I told it to her all,
While the moonbeams on the leaflet
    Left their lines of silver light,
And the katydid was chirping,
    Chirping, calling through the night.

When the days are growing shorter,
    And the leaves are turning red,
And the squirrels drop their acorns
    From the branches overhead—
Then I think of all our rambles,
    And of what we used to say;
For we never tired of talking
    Of our coming wedding day,
Whilst the squirrels dropped their acorns
    From the branches overhead,
When the days were growing shorter,
    And the leaves were turning red.

When the wailing winds of winter
    Moan in mournful monotone,
And, along the dreary woodlands
    I must walk, alas, alone!
Then with longing thoughts I·languish
    For a loved one laid at rest—
Comely arms forever folded,

Folded o'er a snowy breast;
Then my wistful, wooing spirit
Wanders, wailing for its own,
Whilst the wild, weird winds of winter
Moan in mournful monotone.

GONE OUT OF MY LIFE.

Gone out of my life, with her beautiful eyes,
   Those beautiful eyes with their marvelous
      light,
Which flashed o'er my way, as if glanced from
      the skies,
   As meteors shot from the shadows of night!

Gone out of my life, with her delicate lips,
   So temptingly sweet, yet too pure to be
      pressed—
Gone out with their smile, which no gloom
      could eclipse,
   That smile that so mirrored the peace of
      her breast.

Gone out of my life, and she never will know,
   How fond I became of the tones of her voice,
How much of delight to her laughter I owe,
   How her eyes and her smiles have made me
      rejoice.

Gone out of my life, perhaps never to know,
   How restful its waves, while she drifted with
      me,

How softly its tides seemed to ebb and to flow,
How lonely without her the voyage will be.

Gone out of my life, but I cannot forget
   Those eyes and those smiles, and that voice
      that was sweet;
Gone out of my life, yes, forever—and yet—
   God grant that e'en somewhere, bright eyes,
      we shall meet.

Hampton Roads.

"HEN-PECKED."

You charge, that his wife hen-pecks him, John,
   You style her his better half;
You say, that she wears the breeches, John,
   And you swear, it makes you laugh.
You brag, that you are not married, John,
   No slave to petticoat rule,
And claim that you're your own master, John,
   And pity the married fool.

'Tis *you* I sincerely pity, John,
   And all your unmarried gang;
I pity you down in my heart, John,
   In spite of your vulgar slang:
You boast, that you do as you choose, John,
   And go and come as you please,
No anxious wife may await you, John,
   Yet God and your conscience sees.

You are more of a slave to-day, John,
    In love with your wayward life,
Than many a man who follows, John,
    The lead of a loyal wife:
Tho' she walks your home like a queen, John,
    With her love she'll crown you king;
And love is a song that suits her, John,
    A song she delights to sing.

She'll give you her prayers, when you err, John,
    Whilst she feels, she'll not forsake,
She'll bury your fault in her breast, John,
    And smile, tho' her heart should break.
And I hope you'll yet be wedded, John,
    Then, perhaps, you'll understand,
How willingly worn is the yoke, John,
    When touched by a tender hand,

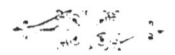

THINE EYES.

TO E. F. W.

As when some watcher scans the evening sky,
  Peers through the far unfathomed blue,
And wonders what new beauties yet may lie
  Beyond the verge of finite view;
Till dazzled by the radiant stars which sail
  Across the amethystine seas,
He looks no longer through the mystic veil,
  But stands entranced, beholding these;

So, sometimes looking in thy soul-lit eyes,
  I try to search their dreamy depths of blue,
To find what secret thought behind them lies,
  And fain would read them through and
    through
Till when they smile—then all the world grows
    bright—
Their light is all the light I see—
Indeed the brightest day would be but night,
  Did they, my stars, not shine for me.

Hampton Roads, Oct. 18, 1889.

MY JEAN AND I.

ON THE ANNIVERSARY OF OUR WEDDING.

I wonder, my sweet, winsome Jean,
  If people question whether
Our hearts have always wedded been,
  Since we joined hands together.
For some have wagged their heads, as though
  No brightness life has brought us;
And some have said * * *—ah, well, we know,
  We know what love has taught us!

We've learned from love, my bonnie Jean,
  To laugh at needless bother;
To stand, through shifting shade and sheen,
  Still steadfast by each other;
To make of life one lasting June
  Of lingering leaf and clover—
Our months one long, sweet honey-moon,
  And me, your loyal lover.

To know no separate joy, my Jean,
  To jointly share our sorrows;
To trust each other, and to lean
  On God for our to-morrows.
So let the world wag on, sweet Jean,
  I shall not care a feather,
So I but walk with you, my queen,
  So we walk on together.

CHECKMATED.

Young Jean and I, one day in June,
  Were loitering on the lawn,
Mamma was napping, for 'twas noon.
  The morning guests had gone;
An open last month's magazine,
  Some bits of wilted flowers
Showed where the merry maids had been—
  How they had passed the hours.

A chess-board lay upon the grass,
  Each piece in proper place,
"Good luck," cried Jean, the cheery lass,
  Then stood with blushing face—
"I challenge you to play," she said,
  "To play a game of chess,"
And turned aside her pretty head,
  Threw back each curling tress.

Then sat we down, and as the grass
  Bent low to touch her feet,
I asked myself "was ever lass—
  Was ever lass so sweet?"
"And now, my gallant Sir," she said,
  "Checkmate me if you can;"
She chose the white, left me the red,
  And then our game began.

       *   *   *   *   *

Forth step my pawns, in red arrayed,
  To strike for king and queen,
White daring knights all undismayed,

Dash boldly in between;
My castles fall before her skill;
   Now one red knight is gone,
She "checks" my fleeing king at will,
   And captures every pawn.

Still stands my queen!   So why despair?
   She's worth a dozen men;
"But hold,"cries Jean,"don't place her there,
   Your king's in check again:
You might have moved your bishops more;
   That blunder seals your fate;
You should have played that knight before;
   The game is mine—checkmate!"

     *   *   *   *   *

"Checkmate?   Ah! well; so let it be,
   It ever ends that way,
You always win the game, you see,
   No matter what we play!
My usual fate!   I do not care,
   So fate no worse befall—
'Tis not the game of life, my dear—
   'Tis by-play after all,

"But in the seige of hearts, sweet Jean,
   Which is for life, you know,
You won mine long ago, my queen,
   You won mine long ago;
Then pity me, your pleading slave,
   Who'd give for you his life,
Confer the only crown I crave—
   The right to call you 'wife.' "

*   *   *   *   *

I know not how it came to pass.
I know I walked in bliss;
The clover grass looked at the lass,
And envied me her kiss.
And since I played that game with Jean,
I've loved her all my life,
Still captive to my charming queen—
Checkmated by my wife.

DREAMING AT DAWN.

THE CONVALESCENT TO HIS WIFE.

The morning, my dearest, was breaking,
The shadows were leaving the lawn,
The mocking-bird, out in the maples,
Was trilling a song to the dawn,
When sleep laid my head on her bosom,
And touching her lips to my eyes,
Allured me away into Dreamland,
Somewhere twixt the earth and the skies.

Far up, through the nebulous ether,
Far up, to the heights of the sky,
Where spirits may mingle together,
Where the lands of the dreamer lie.
No Eden of Houris e'er mirrored
To pious Mohammedan's view
Such beauties as passed me, while dreaming
Of Ethel, of Agnes and you.

Ah, dear me! The visions, my darling,
  I saw 'neath those opaline skies,
While dreaming of you, and of Alice,
  With opiate sleep in my eyes!
I held out my arms unto Ethel
  As she faded away from the scene,
And Agnes, sweet Agnes—I called her—
  But rivers were rolling between.

And some of the faces which charmed me,
  Chamelion-like changed with the skies,
And women with voices of Sirens
  Looked at me through serpent-like eyes;
But Agnes, and Ethel, and Alice—
  You know, I once loved them so much,
And you, dear! But did you not wake me?
  My spirit came back at your touch.

'Twas you then, my darling, who pillowed
  This poor aching brow on your breast,
Who watched in the violet dawning
  Your patient while taking his rest.
What wonder he dreamed of the Houris,
  Of resting in regions of bliss—
'Twas you, who had wooed him to slumber,
  And waked him again with a kiss.

TELL ME, DEAREST, TELL ME.

In your happy girlhood, dearest,
　　In the heyday of your life.
Ere I loved you, ere I wooed you,
　　Ere I won you as my wife;
When you sat beside me, blushing
　　At the boldness of my vow,
Tell me, in your joyous girlhood,
　　Were you happier then than now?

When I longed to be the girdle
　　Clasped so closely round your waist,
And I envied e'en the necklace,
　　Which your peerless throat embraced,
When I loved each little ringlet,
　　Resting lightly on your brow;
In your sunny girlhood, dearest,
　　Were you happier then than now?

When I led you to the altar,
　　And I feared your heart would fail,
As I felt it beating faster,
　　Felt you trembling 'neath your veil,
When they joined our hands together,
　　And you coyly pledged your vow,
In your bridal beauty, tell me,
　　Were you happier then than now?

When I call to mind, my dearest,
　　All the sunlight of your smile,
How your laughter used to lighten
　　Every heavy heart the while,

When I see that time has somewhat
    Left his lines upon your brow—
This it is that makes me ask you,
    Were you happier then than now?

For the tree, if tempest shaken,
    Hurts the ivy 'round it twined,
Wounds it while it loves it dearly,
    Wanting not to be unkind—
Loves each tendril that entwines it,
    Loves each tender leaf and bough—
Thus it is, that I have loved you,
    Loved you through the years till now.

In your happy girlhood, dearest,
    In the heyday of your life,
Ere I loved you, ere I wooed you,
    Ere I won you as my wife,
Ere you met me at the altar,
    Pledging me your wifely vow,
Tell me, oh! my dearest, tell me,
    Were you happier then than now?

A LIFE IN FIVE CHAPTERS.

I.

How brief life's span! It seems but yesterday,
  I saw her clad in swaddling clothes—
A babe upon her mother's breast, she lay
  A perfect picture of repose!

II.

I saw her later on, a laughing lass,
  Brimful of life and loveliness,
And wondered if the time would come to pass,
  When such gay laughter would grow less.

III.

I watched her at the altar, when she stood
  To give to him she loved her hand,
A faultless type of finished womanhood—
  The loveliest lady in the land!

IV.

And next I saw her on her dying bed,
  When life had nothing left but lees,
There was no future way she feared to tread,
  Nor dreaded she Death's mysteries.

V.

I saw sad women with their faces hid,
  As strong-armed men a coffin bore—
I heard dank clods dropped on the casket-lid,
  Then, "Dust to Dust"—and all was o'er!

BY HIS GRAVE.

H. M. C., JR.

Fall lightly on his grave, oh! snow, to-night,
    Fall softly on his grave—
Fit symbol of his soul so pure and white,
    His heart so true and brave.
Like angel tears thy tender drops be shed,
    He was himself so kind;
Light were his faults; peace to the gentle dead,
    To others' faults so blind.

And when Spring comes we'll plant his mound
      with flowers,
    It may be while they grow,
He'll feel their petals falling 'tween the showers,
    In life he loved them so.
And Immortelles, too, about him we'll lay—
    A bunch above his breast,
In token of the Resurrection day—
    And God will do the rest.

Haymarket, Va., Feb. 3, 1897.

JUST FORTY YEARS AGO.

Just forty years ago to-night,
  Just forty years ago,
The chandeliers were shining bright,
  The Yule-logs were aglow;
While forms of beauty, clad in white,
  Were flitting to and fro,
Thro' halls that rung with laughter light,
  Just forty years ago.

And gallant guests had gathered there—
  Ay, men of noble mould
Of Huguenot, and Cavalier,
  Who graced those days of old:
From far and near, the brave and fair,
  Beneath the mistletoe,
Had met to cheer the dying year,
  Just forty years ago.

Ah! me, those merry days of yore,
  Those happy Christmas times,
Which we shall know, ah! never more,
  Unless in poets' rhymes!
What pictures pass before my sight
  Of forms I used to to know!
What visions bright of Christmas night,
  Just forty years ago!

One vision of a woman fair
  How fondly I recall!
Of all the fair the fairest there,
  That graced that festive hall!

And though our paths no more have met,
  Those eyes—they held me so,
I can't forget that look, and yet
  'Twas forty years ago.

I see her standing on the stair,
  Just where she said, "good-bye,"
Then turned away to hide the tear,
  That glistened in her eye:
I feel the pressure of her hand,
  White hand that trembled so—
The dearest hand in all the land,
  Just forty years ago.

Long gone those old ancestral halls—
  The crash of cruel years!
The ivy creeps o'er crumbled walls,
  Where shone those chandeliers:
The owlet hoots where holly hung   .
  Festooned with mistletoe,
Where songs were sung, where laughter rung,
  Just forty years ago.

TO CUPID—AN ACROSTIC.

Let not thy steps, oh! Cupid, come this way;
Unbend thy bow, or pass me by, I pray.
Could Love forget, I'd hail thy shafts with joy,
Yet I must shun them, bold, imprudent boy.

Stay, stay thine hand—an old love holds my
    heart—
Be careful, Cupid, else our paths must part!
Oh, let some love-lorn soul thy darts enshrine!
She must be Queen of Queens who reigns in
    mine.

Why pain the breast Love pierced so deep be-
    fore,
Except thou hold'st some sweeter balm in store!
Lest thine unsated lance impale me, pray,
Let not thy truant footsteps cross my way.

WOMAN'S WORK.

I take it as a true index
Of guilt—I call it by that name—
'Tis guilt, which makes a man defame
　　　His mother's sex.

I pity thee, whoe'er thou art,
Can'st find no worth in woman's ways,
No truth, no trait deserving praise,
　　　No wealth of heart.

Art thou thyself so pure within,
Hast thou no frailties of thine own,
That thou, poor wretch, must cast a stone,
　　　Hast thou no sin?

Hast always walked where weeds have grown,
And passed the purer roses by?
No guileless sister's tender eye
　　　Hast ever known?

Canst thou forget that woman dear,
And all the hopes and fears she felt,
When by thy mother's knee thou'st knelt
　　　In infant prayer?

Or, dearer yet than these—than life—
Hast never felt the perfect bliss,
Which thrills thee in the loving kiss
　　　Of loyal wife?

Dost doubt that woman true can be?

Then win her love, and she will move
The very poles of earth to prove
    Her truth to thee.

Or let her heart be crushed by cares,
Because of thine untruth to trust,
She yet forgives, tho' weep she must
    Whole seas of tears.

When fain in luckless days to fret,
In vain, against the ills of life,
Who girds thee for the stubborn strife,
    Which must be met?

Or, let those friends, who used to fawn
When fortune smiled, now turn away,
Who tells thee of some brighter day,
    Which soon must dawn?

And when, as will, some doubts arise,
Unmanly doubtings of success,
Who holds the victor's happiness
    Before thine eyes?

Or, if some tempting thought within
Thy yielding senses would beguile,
Who leads thee captive to her smile,
    Won back from sin?

'Tis woman does this.   Brave and true,
She nerves thee till the goal is won,
Or cheers thee on, till all is done
    That thou can'st do.

'Tis woman's part—her patient part—
To work, to watch, to pray for thee;
To face her fate, whate'er it be,
    With fearless heart.

To MRS. L. B. W.

INSCRIBED ON THE SAIL OF A BARQUE, PICTURED

ON A NEW YEAR'S CARD.

Go little barque, go bear to her
    Her heart's desires,
Whate'er she deems most dear to her,
    Or most requires;
Sail on, oh! craft, convey to her,
    No cross, no care,
And say what I would say to her
    "A glad new year!"

JUST BEYOND THE BEND.

A BIRTHDAY POEM.

Another mile of life's long journey made,
 Just one more mile-stone nearer to the end!
Look up my soul. Have faith. Be not afraid,
 Our biding place is just beyond the bend.

Sweet resting spot—the weary traveler's last
 relay—
The halt on life's highway we all must make,
Where we can lay aside our garb of clay—
 Lie down to sleep, and in new garments wake!

Not far ahead—one darksome ford between—
 Its stepping-stones are rough, but helpful
 hands
Will hold our own, and angel-forms unseen
 Will lead us upward to the promised lands.

Almost in view. Have faith; a few more days,
 And we shall stand upon the farther shore;
E'en now—I seem to hear sweet strains of
 praise—
Refrains soft chanted, which I've heard be-
 fore.

Remembered voices floating cross the tide,
 Songs sung with dear ones when they came
 to die,
Faint music wafted from the other side,

Familiar songs from lips I've kissed "good-
bye."

Hear them, my soul; hear mingling with them
all
Kind words of comfort to the sore distrest—
Those tones of mercy in the Master's call—
"Come unto me, and I will give you rest."

Another mile of life's long journey made,
Just one more mile-stone nearer to the end;
Look up, my soul! Have faith! Be not afraid!
Our Master waits us just beyond the bend.

NO, NOT GOOD-BYE.

Sweet Alice leaned on the latticed gate
'Neath the moon of the August sky,
And said, "Good-night! It is growing late,
But we must not say 'good-bye,' "
No, not 'good-bye.'

" 'Tis for you to choose, my dear," said I,
"Since I cannot decide it quite—
If you do not love me, then, good-bye!
If you love me, say 'good-night!'
Sweet, say 'good-night.' "

Sweet Alice paused in the gate ajar,
And she blushed 'neath the watching moon;
"Good-bye," she said, "if you're going far!
Good-night, if you're coming soon!
Good-night! Come soon."

POLITICAL.

THE ELECTORAL COMMISSION.

1877.

"This is a surrender, and comes, it is said, from
the South."
—*Donn Piatt in the Washington Capital.*

INSCRIBED TO THE "INVINCIBLE IN PEACE AND

INVISIBLE IN WAR."

Who says that the South, sir, surrenders?
What is it you would have her to do?
You offered to choose her defenders—
She but asked to be guided by you.
With the heel of the despot upon her,
What is it you would have her to give?
They have robbed her of all but her honor,
They have only allowed her to live.

Behold her weighed down by disasters,
Tho' daring—disabled to do!
They have made her own minions, her masters,
Who rivet her fetters anew.
Of what have her foes not bereft her?
You asked for her suffrage—her vote,
Forgetting, when freedom had left her,
The tyrants had throttled her throat.

What advantage her vote, if the rifle
Reverses her verdict of choice—
If fraud and the bayonet stifle
The sound of her people's voice?

Sir, charge not the South with surrender—
    With her—'tis a desperate word;
She has tendered you all she could tender;
    She is looking to you for the sword—

The sword that, if need be, could sunder
    The chains of the tyrant powers;
The guns that, if need be, could thunder
    In tones more effective than ours.
Instead, you proposed "Arbitration,"
    Your remedy of old in disguise,
Your sedative balm for the nation,
    Political curse—"Compromise!"

Then, pardon the South, if she borrow
    A lesson or two from the Past,
You never can fathom the sorrow
    'Neath which her proud people are cast;
She cannot forget how you won her,
    When you promised to stand by the right,
Then trailed all your cannon upon her,
    So soon as she opened the fight.

Oh! taunt her no more with such speeches,
    To her 'tis an ominous word;
The Past of her history teaches
    Surrender only after the sword.
She is used to the clangor of battle—
    Let duty but call her—she comes—
She is used to the musketry's rattle—
    The rattling "long roll" of the drums.

By her dash and her desperate daring,

Wherever her flag was unfurled;
By her deeds and her gallant bearing,
    She challenged the gaze of the world;
Not Greece, in her greatest endeavor,
    Not Rome, in her palmiest age,
No country in history ever
    Illumined so splendid a page!

Heap not your abuses upon her,
    Denounce her not, now, in the dust;
Appomattox was not a dishonor,
    She folded her banners in trust.
Unmanly your charge of surrender,
    She never goes back on her word;
Tho' conquered, her conscience is tender,
    Her honor as bright as her sword!

VIRGINIA DEJECTA.

(Nov. 12th, 1881.)

Virginia, virtuous mother, bowed in shame,
  Shame for the faithless following of those,
Thine own degenerate sons, who bear thy name,
  But fight beneath the banners of thy foes;

Virginia, beauteous mother, bathed in tears,
  Wondrous mother of a once wondrous race,
What baser breed is this thy later years
  Bring forth, to traffic in thine own disgrace?

Virginia, mother, thou hast bent before
  In grief, I know, but never grief like this,
For when thy fullest cup seemed brimming o'er,
  No son betrayed thee with a Judas kiss!

No son of yore did'st lift the tyrant's heel,
  To place it on thy proud but prostrate form;
No hand unfilial pressed the piercing steel,
  To dye it deeper in thy wounds yet warm.

No! never was it said, till now, of old,
  That, leagued with common foes, a son of
    thine,
For love of lucre, or for lust of gold,
  Did'st play the plotting, cunning Catiline.

And when to thy children's children shall be
    read
  The lives of men that make thy name sub-
    lime—

Of Washington and Lee and Jackson dead,
  Whose deeds but brighten with the lapse of
    time,

Then, even will their lisping babes be taught
  To link in one, with false Iscariot's name,
The names of those, who all these wrongs have
    wrought—
  This foul betrayal of Virginia's fame.

"THIS WAY, FREEMEN."

INSCRIBED TO THE HON. MR. NEWBERRY.

Ho! this way, freemen! 'Tis Virginia calls,
  The old State bids you to the field again;
"Hang out our banners on the outward walls!"
  And show the world ye can be, will be men.

Ho! this way, freemen! Hark, she calls once
    more,
  Strike from her shackled limbs the galling
    chain.
Ye never faltered, when she called before,
  And will ye let her call you now in vain?

Ho! this way, freemen! Forward to the front!
  Virginia's desperate struggle is begun,
She bares her bosom to the battle's brunt,
  And asks the help of every honest son.

Ho! this way, freemen!   'Tis no open foe
   Confronts you now, as fronted Jackson bold;
A trusted son hath struck the treacherous blow,
   Iscariot like, for lust of cursed gold.

Ho! this way, freemen!   By *"sic semper"* swear;
   Swear by the sword of dauntless Robert Lee,
That ye a tyrant's yoke will never wear,
   That your revered Virginia shall be free.

Ho! this way, freemen!   Let it not be said
   Virginians lagged when duty led the way;
Remember Pickett's charge o'er mounds of
     dead,
   And say, does lesser cause call you to-day?

Ho! this way, freemen!   If ye will not heed,
   Then never call yourselves Virginians more;
For men will mark you as some mongrel breed,
   Unworthy of the name your fathers wore.

Haymarket, Va., Oct. 19, 1883.

VIRGINIA'S APPEAL TO HER SONS.

Misguided children! sons of honest sires!
   And must it come to this? Your mother's
     heart,
That never nurtured yet but pure desires,
   Compelled to play the shuffling debtor's part?

Your mother's brow, so laurel-wreathed by
     fame,
   That used to flush with pride, to hear the
     praise
Which good men gave, obliged to blush with
     shame,
   Because her sons keep not in virtue's ways?

Virginia, mother of a once proud race—
   No nobler known upon the tide of time—
To hear the story of her own disgrace,
   The vulgar jest of clowns of every clime!

Immortal spirits of her statesmen great!
   Would that these sons were of your finer
     mould!
Virginia fallen from her high estate,
   And all for paltry sums of borrowed gold!

Deluded sons, your luckless steps retrace,
   Your mother begs you on her bended knee;
Virginia must resume her wonted place,
   The brightest in her country's galaxy.

Yea! By those deeds ye did in days of yore—

Those lustrous deeds which fame has set to
    song,
My children, pause! Virginia may be poor,
  But is not poor enough to stoop to wrong.

January 20, 1887.

THE BOURBON'S REPLY.

LADY—"Are you a Bourbon, sir?"

Am I a "Bourbon," madam?   Yes, thank God!
  I grant I am, and glory in the name;
And were I not, my fathers, 'neath the sod,
  Would shudder in their tombs for very shame!
Go, read Virginia's living roll of fame,
  See who is numbered with the good and great,
Each line illumined by some Bourbon's name,
  Some scion worthy of the dear old State!

I care not, madam, what the word may mean,
  Or how the scholars use it; but I know
No man, who always hath a Bourbon been,
  Is ever counted as his country's foe.
If, madam, by the word you mean a man
  Who guards his honor as he guards his life,
Who dares do all that conscious courage can,
  Nor strikes his colors till he tries the strife;

If Bourbon be a man who, true to trust,
  Before dishonor would prefer to die,
Who would not trail his banner in the dust,

Tho' forced by fate to fold that banner by;
Who loves his country, and obeys her laws,
Who counts Virginia's glory as his own,
And dares refuse to follow in the cause
Of those who would her honest debts disown;

If men of Gordon's, Hill's, and Hampton's
    mould,
If men like Bayard, Butler, and Lamar,
Who follow still the fathers' faith of old—
If patriots such as these all Bourbons are;
If these be Bourbons, madam, these good men—
And need I, madam, need I tell you why?
I only say, if these be Bourbons, then
    I am a Bourbon of the deepest dye!

But some there are, "would rather reign in hell
    Than serve in heaven"—ay, men of meaner
    mould—
Time-serving mongers, who would stoop to sell
    Their honor and themselves for paltry gold!
Who sneer at all the virtues of the past,
    Who scorn the teachings of the olden time,
But who shall stand before the world at last
    As rude abettors in the cause of crime!

See, madam, how our good old ship of State
    Strains all her beams, with pirates at her
    · helm,
Who swear in wrath to rule or wreck her fate,
    And wreak their vengeance on the ancient
    realm!
Then mark me as a Bourbon—ay, indeed!

And tho' bad men may mock, and fools may
  laugh,
Yet when I die, oh! may my children read
"He was a Bourbon!" as my epitaph.

Haymarket, Va., Oct. 16, 1882.

VIRGINIA REDEMPTA.

A JUBILEE.

Virginians, unfurl your famed banner of old,
Your motto, *sic semper tyrannis*, unfold,
And tell ye the tidings, wherever ye be,
That Washington's birth-place is once again
  free.

Yea, tell it, ye people, from mouth unto mouth,
Proclaim it aloud to the North, to the South,
That Jefferson's country, from mountain to sea,
The mother of States and of statesmen, is free.

Proclaim to the world, how ye rose in your
  might,
As heroes of old, in defence of the right,
And swore by the sword of your chivalrous Lee,
Your dear Old Dominion must ever be free.

Proclaim how ye smote him, who traitor to
  trust,
Was trampling his motherland down in the
  dust;

Sic semper tyrannis, so may it e'er be
To him, who would barter the rights of the free.

Proclaim it, ye poets, proclaim it in song,
How thousands arose in resistance to wrong,
Resolved in their hearts, that Virginia should be
The land of all others, the home of the free.

Ay! fling to the breeze your famed banner of
    old,
Your legend, *sic semper tyrannis*, unfold;
Proclaim the glad tidings from mountain to sea,
Virginia redempta—Virginia is free.
Haymarket, Va.

THANKSGIVING.

Nov. 27, 1884.

Oh! Thou eternal Ruler, Judge supreme,
    We give Thee thanks, that Thou, oh! King
        of kings,
On us, at last, hast let thy presence beam;
    We thank Thee for the joy that presence
        brings.

We thank Thee for the hope, that strife shall
    cease,
    And quiet reign, and factious leagues disband;
We thank Thee for the trust, that palmy peace
    Shall henceforth tarry in this troubled land.

We thank Thee, Lord, that Thou did'st shape
    our fate,
    E'en whilst the waves did well-nigh over-
      whelm;
That Thou did'st safely moor our ship of state,
    And call our chosen pilot to the helm;

That Thou did'st hear us, Lord, when sore dis-
    tressed;
    And when our sinking ship began to fill;
That Thou did'st walk upon the waters' breast,
    That Thou did'st bid the stormy sea be still.

We thank Thee, too, that this, our own dear
    land,
    Virginia, birth-place of the brave and free,
Once more, among the States shall proudly
    stand,
    Torn from the tyrant's grasp, our God, by
      Thee.

Accept our thanks, Jehovah, God, we pray,
    Accept our thanks, oh! Lord, Thou King of
      kings,
Accept our thanks, for this long looked for day,
    For all the hopes and happiness it brings.

WAR.

LEE'S WELCOME.

COLUMBIA, S. C., MARCH 30, 1870.

All day the murky clouds hung low
  Above the silent city;
The skies seemed draped in robes of woe—
  To weep in very pity—
In pity for our wounded pride,
  In pity for our people,
While, since the dawn the winds had sighed
  'Round crumbling tower and steeple.

The wrecks of old ancestral halls,
  In all their desolateness,
The ruined walks and blackened walls
  To foeman's hate bore witness.
Against the sky the toppling stacks
  In solemn, sad sedateness,
Seemed sentries on their beaten tracks—
  Grim ghosts of former greatness.

Each sombre mart deserted seemed,
  The day wore dull and dreary,
While men moved on, as men that dreamed,
  With footsteps flagging weary.
But, hark! that sudden clamor hear!
  That hum of human voices!
Whilst everywhere, with shout and cheer,
  The very air rejoices.

One little word, first faintly heard,
  Now thousands echo loudly,

And every Southern heart is stirred,
  And every head held proudly!
Maimed men and matrons shout—"'Tis Lee!"
  Fair maidens swell the chorus;
The children clap their hands in glee;
  The sky grows brighter o'er us.

'Tis he! 'tis he! the hero Lee!
  No hostile sword can sever
Our hearts from him, for he shall be
  The sovereign of them ever.
The tidings leap from street to street,
  Each tongue that name repeating,
And many meet with hastening feet
  To give the hero greeting.

See how the brave old chieftain comes—
  No banners o'er him soaring;
No roll is heard of mighty drums,
  No cannons 'round him roaring.
On every heart himself engraved,
  What need of laurelled arches?
'Neath lifted hats and kerchiefs waved
  Our gray-haired warrior marches.

When in the Christian cause of peace
  His sword was sheathed forever,
With him we wept, that we must cease
  Our brave but vain endeavor;
And still we love him as of old,
  When 'mongst the dead and dying,
He rode the boldest of the bold,
  Our foe before him flying.

Ah! 'twas a splendid sight to see
  Our Southern chiefs assembled
To greet their grand old leader, Lee,
  'Fore whom once foemen trembled!
And though our flag be furled—yet we
  Forget our heroes never:
We can but shout, "Long live our Lee!"
"The South and Lee forever!"

THE SOUTHERN FLAGS.

Let those flags be furled forever,
  Just as when we laid them down,
Emblems of a vain endeavor,
  Duty done without its crown.
Covered as they are with glory,
  Let them moulder into dust,
Emblematic of their story,
  Emblematic of our trust.

Let those braves who charged upon them,
  Men who met us in the fight;
They who by their valor won them,
  Let them keep them—theirs by right.
Let them keep them, torn and tattered,
  Tokens of the tears they cost;
Symbols of a people scattered,
  Emblems of the cause they lost.

Emblems of a people dashing
  Down the tide of Time to die;
Meteor-Like, in splendor flashing,

Flaming 'cross the Southern sky!
When before did any nation,
  Born of only hopes and prayers,
Freely offer such libation,
  Pouring out its blood and tears?

Not old Rome's heroic ages;
  Not e'en Greece's grandest days;
Not the world's historic pages,
  Furnish such a theme for praise.
Classic Greece yet tells the deeds of
  Heroes of her land and sea;
Wondering, all the world now reads of
  Raphael Semmes and Robert Lee.

Never marched men into battle,
  Braver men with firmer tread,
Spite of all the roar and rattle,
  Spite of dying and the dead.
Rest, ye warriors, from your labors;
  Rest your banners worn to rags;
Sheathed forever are your sabres,
  Furled forever be your flags.

Though in vain our brave endeavor,
  Though our skies be overcast,
Appomattox meant "forever,"
  No repinings for the past.
Symbols of a grand oblation,
  Keep those flags forever furled,
Emblems of a vanished nation,
  Once the wonder of the world.

Haymarket, Va., July 4, 1887.

SHE WEEPS FOR HER DEAD.

A voice of distress, as if Rachaels were weeping!
The gloom of a sorrow o'ershadows the land!
A funeral dirge through the Southland is
 sweeping,
From Chesapeake bay to the far Rio Grande!
The South is in tears! And from tower and
 from steeple
She tolls to the nations how deep is her
 grief—
Her Davis is dead—whilst her millions of people,
 Men, maidens and matrons, are mourning
 their chief!

Kind Nature herself, her green garland is
 wreathing,   .
 White roses are dropping their redolent
 bloom,
Magnolias their sweetest of incense are breathing,
 Where, weeping, the Southland bends over
 his tomb;
She weeps, the South weeps, with her waters
 that quiver;
 She droops with the mosses that trail from
 her trees;
She mingles her. sighs with the sough of the
 river,
 Which sobs on its way by his home to the
 seas.

She weeps, aye, she weeps in her wonderful
  beauty!
She weeps, but no tears of a guilty regret;
She followed her faith; never faltered at duty;
  She weeps for her dead, whom she cannot
  forget;
She mourns her great captain, whose fame is
  her glory,
  Who, loyal to conscience, passed under the
  rod;
She asks but for justice in telling her story,
  And leaves her lost cause and its leader to
  God.

Fortress Monroe, Va., Dec. 11, 1889.

THE LEE STATUE, UNVEILED.

MAY 29, 1890.

Though Victory crowneth not thy brow,
  Thou stand'st to-day, unveiled,
Type of the manliest manhood, thou,
  That ever fighting, failed.
Well may'st thou hold aloft thy head;
  Immortal is its crown;
And though the cause thou led'st be dead,
  Deathless is thy renown!

'Twas thine to stand against the world,
  'Gainst race of every name;
And though thy battle-flag be furled,
  'Tis wreathed with fadeless fame.
No braver soul e'er dared be free,
  Or stood in strife more stern!
Not Spartan at Thermopylæ,
  Not Scott at Bannockburn!

Nor ever shall thy memory die,
  While tongue or pen can tell
Of daring deeds, of purpose high,
  For which thy comrades fell;
And so in story thou shalt stand,
  In legend and in lore,   ·
The idol of thy native land,
  Till time shall be no more.

THE MEN OF MECKLENBURG.

RESPECTFULLY INSCRIBED TO THE CONTINENTAL
GUARDS, COMMANDED BY HERIOT CLARKSON,
AT THE UNVEILING OF THE MONUMENT
AT CHARLOTTE, N. C., MAY 20, 1898.

Draw near, ye worthy sons of daring sires,
 And ye, sweet daughters of the Old North
  State,
Come, mingle with us 'round our council fires,
 And hear the wondrous story we relate.

Ay, come ye Carolinians, old and young,
 Come, list a chapter from the Book of Time,
As grand a theme as ever yet was sung,
 The simple story of a deed sublime.

Give ear, how years ago, one morn of May,
 The men of Mecklenburg, on bended knee,
Threw off the galling yoke of Britain's sway,
 And swore that their dear Province must be
  free;

How six and twenty spirits tried and true,
 Each armed with burnished gun or belted
  sword—
The dauntless Polk, and Phifer, Patton, too,
 The Alexanders, Avery, Reese and Ford,

And Barry, Irwin, Query and McClure,
 The Harrises and Wilson, heroes all,
Each heart resolved no longer to endure

Insulting foe, though death itself befall;

With Graham, Kennon, Downs and Flenniken,
   And Morrison and Balch, and brave Brevard,
From each train-band two firm and fearless
      men,
   With Captain Jack and Davidson on guard,

In face of foes, in spite of hostile laws,
   Had rendezvoused in this Old Charlotte Town,
And pledging life and fortune in their cause,
   Abjured allegiance to the English crown.

What time their land a warlike aspect wore,
   And Tryon's hirelings every hamlet filled,
These men as "Regulators" years before,
   On banks of Alamance their blood had spilled.

And now, once more have picked their idle
      flints,
   Again have put their rested armor on,
Closed up their ranks, flung out their banners
      since
   The news of fighting at far Lexington.

Not yet had Patrick Henry's voice been heard
   In "Give me liberty or give me death,"
Yet Independence was the magic word,
   Which leapt from tongue to tongue on every
      breath.

No chief commander had been chosen yet,
   Nor Jefferson's bold Magna Charter passed,
And though the people's Congress just had met,

Alone, old Mecklenburg the die had cast.

Not strange that sound of fife and drum was
    heard,
The tread of tramping horse for miles around,
That Independence every bosom stirred,
    And Mecklenburg was all one battle ground.

Not strange that Lord Cornwallis, baffled foe,
    Should find in Charlotte Town "a hornet's
    nest,"
That wily Ferguson should fear it so,
    And Tarleton damn it as "a rebel pest."

Methinks, I see the Muse of History pause,
    With finger pointed to a famous page—
To names of those, who in their country's
    cause,
    Have made illustrious their land and age.

And when was record of a knightlier deed,
    Than that of Davie dashing down the glen,
In front of Charlotte Town, to take the lead,
    In counter-charging Tarleton's mounted men?

What finer picture than heroic Locke,
    The leader of a small but daring band,
Drawn out in line, to meet the battle shock
    Of fourteen hundred foemen, hand to hand?

And though they fight as few have fought be-
    fore,
    He drives them back o'er hollow and o'er hill,
Defeats the Tory bands of Welsh and Moore,

And gives a deathless name to Ramseur's
Mill.

Who hath not heard of Gaston's gallant sons,
Who kneeling, kissed their father's naked
sword,
And swore they never would lay down their
guns,
While one is left of all the British horde?

Aye, this the spirit—meeting blow with blow—
A spirit born of stern Scotch-Irish stock,
Which put to rout the proud exulting foe,
And won the stubborn field of Hanging Rock.

And this the sentiment which nerved McLeod,
Which roused the heroes, Rutherford and
Nash,
Which fired young Graham and his gallants
proud,
To follow where they heard the sabres clash.

Such, Carolinians, were those sires of yours,
Who bore your banners to the breeze un-
furled,
Who drove the British foe beyond your shores,
And gave a new born nation to the world.

Small wonder then when four-score years had
passed,
And fiercer foes were thundering at your
shores,
Your patience under wrongs gave way at last,

With war's rude touch upon your very doors!

What wonder that in Eighteen-Sixty-One,
   Such rightful thoughts should every bosom
      fill,
That principles bequeathed by sire to son,
   Should then declare for Independence still.

Not strange that Vance and Ransom, through
      whose hearts
   Such rich blood circled back and forth again;
Not strange that they should act so well their
      parts,
   Those proud descendants of such princely
      men!

And we, who saw your men at Malvern Hill,
   And marked their gallantry in every fight,
The charge they made at bloody Gaines's Mill,
   The sturdy blows they struck for home and
      right;

Who heard their cheers and loud triumphant
      shouts,
   As Iverson and Meares, advancing fast,
Drove Porter back beyond his strong redoubts,
   And turned the tide of battle at the last;

Who heard their welcome cry of victory sound,
   And saw their serried ranks, at Seven Pines,
While shot and shrapnel plowed the trembling
      ground,
   As gallant Garland led their charging lines;

Yes, we who watched your comrades under
  Hill,
Their colors frontward borne on every field,
We felt they fought for Independence still—
  Proud spirits, who would rather die than
  yield.

Then skyward raise your gray memorial shaft,
  Your graceful column to the world unveil,
And let high heaven itself its moral waft,
  Its stirring epic on the passing gale.

And when your children's children stop to read
  The names engraven on its granite base,
Inform them of their fathers' famous deed—
  The daring action of a dauntless race.

And let your people set apart this day,
  Forever keep its memories alive,
Keep holy this, the twentieth day of May,
  This sacred date of Seventeen-Seventy-Five.

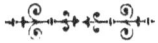

To COLUMBIA VICTRIX. ‾

AUGUST 12, 1898.

Now let thy conquering flags be furled,
  Thy calls to battle cease;
Teach thou the people of the world
  The pleasantness of peace.
No nation now but knows thy might—
  Thy strength on land and sea;
The world in wonder watched thy fight,
  And cheered thy chivalry.

All praise to Hobson and to Schley,
  Praise to their brave commands,
To Shafter's gallant slain, who lie
  'Neath Santiago's sands:
Yet weep with those, who weep in Spain
  O'er blood thyself hast shed—
Weep, though the tears be wept in vain,
  Weep for Cervera's dead.

The God who said, "Thou shalt not kill,"
  Has not revoked His word,
But emphasizing still His will,
  Commands, "Put up thy sword."
Then learn Christ's lesson, "To forgive"—
  From wars forever cease—
Teach thou the nations how to live
  In universal peace.

JIM AND JOE.

IN THE WILDERNESS.

"Tell us a tale like you told befo',"
Says Georgia Jim to Virginia Joe,
"But none of your yarns, like them you told
'Bout Grant a-payin' his Yanks in gold."

And each draws closer beside the fire,
Whilst comrades pile on the fagots higher.
What! Tears are they, which they brush away,
Those two brave men, in their rags of gray?

"Well, boys," says Joe, "I'll jus' tell you what,
They may git their pay in gold, or not,
But I b'lieve them Yanks would jus' refuse
To march at all in our green-hide shoes!"

"But they are fightin' for pay, you see,
While we enlis' jus' for Gen'ral Lee;
That makes a diff'rence, of course, you know—
Jim, quit your braggin' 'bout Longstreet so.

"You know, no man on the army roll
Can tetch Marse Bob with a ten-foot pole;
An' even ole Abe, himself, they say,
Is afeard he'll fight till the judgment day."

"Yes, Joe, I reckon you're right," says Jim,
"Them Yanks would lick us, if 'twan't for
    him"— ·
"Then own," adds Joe, "what I said befo',
Marse Bob is the grandest man you know.

"You recollec' what the cap'en said,
'Just keep Marse Bob at the army's head,
An' we'll lick the world, and Yankees, too?'
Well, 'pon my word, I believe it's true.

"I'll tell you, boys, what I hearn 'em say
About Marse Bob jus' the other day,
'Twas when we camped on the old Stone-pike,
An' we all was sort o' starvin' like—

" 'Twas 'bout the time, you remember, Jim, .
Grant was a-plannin' to tackle him—
That fighter they fetched from out the Wes',
To meet Marse Bob in the Wilderness.

"Some Richmon' cit'zens had come to see
What news they could git from Gen'ral Lee,
An' all, a-settin' aroun' on rocks,
Was dinin' off of a dry-goods box.

"An' what do you think they had to eat?
A mess of pease an' a piece o' meat,
But none of them gents would tetch a bite
Off o' that meat, they were so perlite!

"Well, nex' day Marse Bob set down to dine,
An' axed his man for that tender-line,
But the darkey stopped, an' scratched his head,
An' hem'd an' haw'd, an', at las', he said,

" 'Dat meat, Marse Bob, nebber b'longed to us,
Trufe is, 'twas loant to the mess on truss,
Done sont it back whar I got it from—

Borrerd it, sar, from the Chaplain's Tom.'

"Now that is the Gen'ral's way," adds Joe,
"Meat twice a week, is his rule, you know,
He fares no better than we do, boys,
And hasn't always what we enjoys.

"But the doctors say, 'he ought to take
Meat every day for his stomach's sake'—
Yet, 'No,' says he, 'for the men have none,
And I can do jus' as they have done.'

" 'Totes a canteen ?'   Yes, but jus' to think,
He never tetches a drop to drink!
'When fightin' ?'   No, but be fills it then
With home-made wine for the wounded men.

"But boys, don't you know, them Yanks git
          drunk,
'Least their head men do, to keep up spunk,
But Marse Bob jus' fights without, you know,
And that's one reason we lick 'em so."

"Now, don't be braggin' yourself," says Jim,
"For Grant, they say, is a match for him;
And never counts what the battles cost,
Nor cares a cent for the lives that's lost."

"I don't dispute it," says Joe, with pride,
"But God stan's up for the prayin' side;
I know, that Grant has plenty o' men—
The fightenest sort, I 'low, but then,

"You wait till you see Marse Bob take off
His ole slouch hat, with its plume alof',
His lips mayn't move, but he's prayin' then
To God to defen' his bare-foot men.

"Jus' wait till you see him wave his han',
An' say to Longstreet, 'you take comman'—
If never befo' you've hearn that shout,
You'll think the devil himself was out."

And thus they talk, till the morning drum
Tells that danger with the day has come.
Soon couriers are dashing to and fro,
"Fall in—fall in," orders sergeant Joe.

"The long-roll's a-beatin'!   Listen boys!
Blood's on the sky, when you hear that noise;
Marse Bob is boun' for the Wilderness,
To lick that man, like he licked the res'."

* * * * * *

But Grant sits his horse in silence grim,
And all his men are "in fighting trim"—
Two-hundred thousand, the very best
Equipped, and fresh from a winter's rest.

Shall force so feeble, so small as Lee's,
One-fourth their number, contend with these?
Ay! what care they, for Marse Bob commands,
And God, they believe, upholds his hands.

And now, once more, the Blue and the Gray
Confront each other in fierce array:
Weep, women, weep!   'Tis a fearful shock,

When North and South their bayonets lock!

See, Hancock pushing his splendid corps,
Blazing his pathway with human gore,
Whilst dead and dying lie heaped around,
Like leaves of Autumn, bestrew the ground!

Shouts rend the clouds, as the gray line swerves
In falling back on its rear reserves,
Then parts in twain, whilst the hosts in blue
Sweep like an avalanche, charging through.

But Longstreet sees them, and quick as thought,
His ragged braves from the rear has brought,
Riding abreast of his boys in gray,
He moves them up to the bloody fray.

Now, just for a moment, face to face,
The North and South, of the self-same race,
Glare at each other with years of hate,
Whilst 'twixt them quivers the scale of fate.

Will never those Northmen yield an inch?
Will never those Southrons flee nor flinch,
As Longstreet, leading his line of gray,
Stubbornly strives for the right of way?

Ha! see! he stands in his stirrups, then,
"Forward," he orders—"March steady, men!
Now up, and at them, and let them feel
What you can do with the naked steel!"

And when was a grander charge e'er made;

When was commander so well obeyed,
As 'bove the dust and the battle's noise,
Ascend the shouts of those shoeless boys ?

See! shoulder to shoulder, Jim and Joe
Are double-quicking against the foe—
"Hurrah!" cried Joe, "Look! the Yankees
    break"—
"Let's crowd 'em," says Jim, "for Longstreet's
    sake!"

"Three cheers for Lee!" calls Virginia Joe,
"The Lord is answerin' his prayers, you know."
"Hurrah! for Longstreet!" shouts Georgia Jim,
"For surely we owe this all to him."

And Longstreet, exultant, stops to shake
Jim's sun-burned hand for acquaintance sake,
Then dashes on, when a louder shout
Strikes his keen ear, as he wheels about.

A burst of smoke from the thickets nigh,
And whizzing the whistling bullets fly!
"Halt! Cease firin' there! my God," cries Joe,
"Them's our men, Gen'ral, what's firin' so."

"What! Wounded ? Blood, sir ? Blood on your
    sleeve!
Mistook us for Yanks, I do believe!"
But Longstreet reels, and his senses swim,
He falls in the faithful arms of Jim.

Borne from the field by his men away,

The foe emboldened, renews the fray—
Already the news has reached the rear—
Lo! Lee like a king comes riding there!

See, what a majestic mien he wears,
As full to the breeze his brow he bares;
With lips firm set, and his eyes aglow,
Points his finger to the daring foe!

Halts for a moment where Longstreet lies,
Stifling the tears which bedew his eyes,
Then mutters a prayer, as is his wont,
And spurs his horse to the very front!

But what man there, but would rather be
Dead on the field, than that Robert Lee
Should be hurt by hostile shot, or shell?
Sooner would he storm the gates of hell!

A dozen stout men have stepped betwixt
Those battling lines, with bayonets fixed,
Each resolute breast, and brawny arm,
Determined to guard Marse Bob from harm.

See gallant Gordon soon takes the lead,
Turns about, and checks his charging steed,
Throws himself athwart his chieftain's path,
Thus to shield him from the battle's wrath!

"Gen'ral Lee to the rear!" hear him cry,
"Let him be safe, if we all must die!"
"Gen'ral Lee to the rear!" shout they all,
"He must be saved, tho' we all should fall."

And Joe, too, seizing the Gen'ral's bit,
Pleads, "pray, go back, for you may git hit;
An' we'll promise you, yes, every man—
We'll drive them Yanks to the Rapidan."

Touched by the love which his men display,
Lee reins his horse, and has turned away;
Then rings the brave Gordon's voice again—
"Forward, Virginians!   Remember men,

The promise you've made Marse Bob to-day—
Forward!   Georgians, march!   We'll hew the
        way!"
Then right from their ranks resounds a yell,
That seems to swell from the depths of hell.

Now, never was field more quickly won,
Never was duty more nobly done;
Like trees, when felled by the tempest's breath
Ten thousand foemen lie down in death!

God must have listened to Robert Lee,
Praying that He would their leader be,
For the blue line melts before the gray,
Like fleeing mists at the break of day.

EVELYN.

EVELYN.

I.

Of wild, of warlike times I tell, long years
Of patient hopes, and soul-impassioned prayers,
Sad years of cruel strife and vengeful hate,
Sad days decisive of a people's fate.
But sadder yet the subject of my song—
A strange wild tale of grief, of private wrong,
Of spirits brave, defiant of the foe,
Tho' crushed to earth beneath their weight of
        woe—
A tale of daring and of deeds sublime,
No grander graven in the book of time—
A tale of love—of woman's love, its tears,
Its fond, delightful doubts, its hopes, its fears,
Its thousand tender thoughts, its smiles, its
        sighs,
And all its anxious, secret sympathies.

But erst to earlier times, ere war's rude hand
Had wrought disaster on our Southern land;
Ere foe had passed Potomac's peaceful waves,
To make our homes sad homes of tear-wet
        graves,
To halcyon days of old, when far and wide
His fruitful fields the farmer's wealth supplied,
When yellow harvests smiled, when pastures
        green,
And peace and plenty everywhere were seen.

Where grows the cypress and the sighing pine,

Where climbs the closely clinging columbine,
And tall magnolias cast their cooling shades
'Mid myrtle groves and greenest everglades;
Where flowers know not the snowy shrouds of
    death,
Or icy winter with its withering breath,
Where perfumes kiss the bosom of the earth,
And nature smiles, and beauty has its birth—
There on a mild and summer-scented morn,
By Eutaw's banks was Albert Ashleigh born—
'Mong Carolina's hills his infant eyes
First caught the blue and splendor of the skies,

    In wealth's luxurious lap he lay and smiled,
His doting parents' first and only child,
Their link of love, their idol and their pride;
Nor means, nor pains were spared, nor plans
      untried
To make him worthy of the name he bore,
As proud a name as peer or prince e'er wore.
Of gentle blood begot, this boy, in truth,
Grew up a goodly and a gallant youth.

    Just at that tender April-time of life,
When boyhood's heart with budding feelings
      rife,
Untouched by thought of winter's later gloom,
Is gliding into youth's soft summer bloom,
When strange new sentiments incite the breast,
And all the senses feel a sweet unrest—
'Twas at such yearning age young Albert met
A kindred spirit he could ne'er forget—
A spirit beaming out from eyes so bright,

The very stars grew pale within their light.
You need but note that face so passing fair,
That modest grace, that mien so debonair,
The rich, soft music of those accents mild,
To know Virginia claimed that beauteous child.

Where limpid Massaponax lightly laves
The hills of Spottsylvania with its waves,
Where round a sloping lawn its waters glide
To join with Rappahannock's deeper tide,
Upon its banks embosomed in the wood,
Young Evelyn's mansion-home, Glen Arvon,
    stood;
'Neath nodding elms and maple's silver sheen,
Its ivied porch and graceful gables seen,
Its terraced roads 'twixt banks of blooming
    rose,
Its gravelled walks, by which sweet flowers
    repose,
Its friendly open door, its larder stored,
Its cheerful hearth, and hospitable board,
Its countless comforts to the mind suggest
Virginia welcome to the greeted guest.

Yet not in this ancestral home, so sweet,
Did Albert and the guileless Evelyn meet,
But far across the wide Atlantic's roar,
Afar beyond her dear Virginia's shore,
Beneath the blue of love-enkindling skies,
Where love once born, burns deep, but never
    dies—
In climes of classic lore and heroes grand,
Italia's cultured homes and smiling land.

In Florence, on a summer's afternoon,
One dreamy day of blossom-dropping June,
With thoughtful brow, and kindling eye intent,
A Tuscan painter o'er his pallet bent.
Thro' patient toil this artist had portrayed
The perfect picture of a peerless maid.
The blending colors on his canvas beamed
So like to living tints, it almost seemed,
As if the lace-edged bodice rose and fell
With every movement of the bosom's swell.
'Twas Leonardo Vecchi's magic brush,
Which made those features seem to pale and
    flush,
Those velvet lips to part, almost to speak,
And smiles to dimple on the damask cheek.
Beneath the blueness of those soul-lit eyes,
Whose hues his brush had borrowed from the
    skies,
Old Leonardo lingered, till their glow
Awaked sweet memories of the long ago.

And late he labored to depict each charm,
Then leaned his head upon his weary arm,
And gazing on the work his hand had wrought,
He vainly strove to crush the rising thought—
One thought indelible of days gone by—
A life-long memory, which would not die,
Till weary nature, watchful of her claim,
Enwrapped in gentle sleep his aged frame.
In dreams he lives his happy boyhood o'er,
He looks into his Lucia's eyes once more,
Nor heeds he now the opening of the door,

The studied, noiseless step across the floor,
Nor sees his faithful pupil near him stand,
Till lightly touched by Albert's friendly hand,
He wakes, and troubled, starting from his
    dreams,
His gray locks glistening in the sunset beams,
He anxious asks: "And thou art come, my boy!
Hast seen her, Albert, and dost bring me joy?"
Does Lucia live? Hast left her at Lausanne—
Or lies she ill, a stranger, in Milan?
Go, bring her, boy! Go, tell her she must come
With husband, Evelyn, all to share my home,
And say, 'tis Leonardo begs the bliss,
The playmate of her girlhood asks her this."

Then answers Albert: "Sire, be quiet now;
Too oft, of late, hath fever flushed that brow;
So come—I pray thee, do not labor late,
Our galley waits us at the garden gate."

"Stay, Albert, I was dreaming, ere you came,
Of days gone by, ere this old shattered frame
Had bent with age. Methought, a youth, once
    more,
I walked along the Adriatic's shore
With one, who then was hardly more than child,
And yet I loved her with a love as wild,
As those rough waters rushing o'er yon reef,
Arno's rude mockery of mortal grief.
How oft my hours of boyhood were beguiled
By Lucia's smiles! And yet she never smiled
Whene'er I talked of love! The years wore
    on—

Long years to one, whose light of life was gone;
In vain I worshipped at another shrine;
In vain I thought to drown my woes in wine;
I cursed, at last, my fate, and followed fame,
Meanwhile from o'er the seas a stranger came—
A pleasing youth, who won my Lucia's hand,
And took her with him to his far-off land.
He was thy countryman, my boy, and none
Denied him worthy of the love he won.
Full many a flying year since then hath passed
With Lethe on its wings, and time, at last,
Hath   lightened   disappointment's   poignant
      pains,
And friendship only now for her remains.
'Tis told that Lucia lived in easy wealth,
Nor lost the fullness of her blooming health,
Till two hard winters gone, a flowery flush
Came o'er   each   fair   white   cheek—a   hectic
      blush—
The   kiss   of   wan   Consumption's   wasting
      breath—
The rosy trophies of triumphant death.
As seeks some tropic bird, in winter time,
The warmer shelter of its native clime,
So Lucia left her home across the sea
For milder skies, her own sweet Italy.
Her ills beyond the skill of mortal man,
In early spring I saw her in Milan,
Her husband, anxious, bending o'er her couch,
As Evelyn soothed her with her softest touch.
We watched her wasted form and wan white
      cheek;

Her faint smile made me weep. I heard her
    speak
From pale, sweet lips—her lustrous, lovely eye
Illumed with light of Immortality.''

As Leonardo turns to hide a tear,
His pupil speaks: "Sire, pardon me, but there
Upon that breathing canvas thou hast set
A face, it seems not easy to forget;
The more its faultless, faithful lines I scan,
The more methinks, I have seen it in Milan.''

"Aye, likely, boy! 'Tis Lucia's matchless
    face,
And yet in Lucia now, 'twere hard to trace
That rounded fullness and that girlish grace.
From memory, boy, that beauty I impart,
The fadeless memory of a faithful heart.
'Twas thus she once upon my pathway smiled—
As such I loved her then—a laughing child;
With that sweet face the hours I have beguiled
And gazing on it, fondly gazing, dreamed—
A sudden deathly pallor o'er it seemed
To spread—anon, a smile, as angels wear,
In momentary splendor lingered there:
Methought it moved—and then a whisper said,
'Alas! Leonardo—thy Lucia's dead!' ''

The old man paused and sighing, turned
    away,
As Albert answered: "Sire, 'twas but the play
Upon thy canvas of the dying day—
The flushing of the sunset's parting beams—

And yet—that voice—who knows? It some-
    times seems
Love's sweetest messages are sent in dreams!
Who knows but Jacob's ladder still may lean
Against the azure wall of Heaven, unseen,
By which the angel-couriers come and go—
Some, messengers of weal, and some, of woe?
We hear a voice, and tho' no shape appears,
We entertain an angel unawares;
And Sire—to-day, about the eventide,
The loved one of thy life—thy Lucia died."

      *   *   *   *   *

'Tis morning in Milan; the great cathedral's
    ponderous gate,
And iron doors, now harshly on their heavy
    hinges grate:
With muffled, measured tread, in saddened
    march, a mournful few
Are slowly moving onward thro' the light be-
    spangled dew;
A funeral-bell hath early tolled its tones of
    deep despair,
Its doleful sullen dirge hath died upon the
    startled air;
The hollow throats of organs peal their brazen
    notes—the while,
A cortege bears a coffined form along the
    lengthy aisle,
And softly, with the incense, to the stuccoed
    ceiling floats
A sweet harmonic melody of slowly chanted
    notes:

What tho' the loved form lieth 'neath the
  cold and cheerless sod,
We know the spirit flieth to the bosom of its
  God;

What tho' our bodies perish—earth to earth,
  and dust to dust!
Are there not hopes to cherish—fondest hopes
  in which to trust?

Mourn not the dear departed, for in death there
  is no sting,
Look up, ye broken-hearted! Lo, the cross to
  which we cling!

·What tho' the loved form lieth in the grave's
  polluting breath
We know the soul defieth all that thou can'st
  do, oh, death!

  * * * * *

Sepulchral Psalms and choral chants have
  ceased their sounds o'erhead,
The surpliced priest hath read the solemn
  ritual of the dead,
Now friendly mourners slowly step behind that
  sable bier,
Whilst Evelyn, at her father's side, conceals
  the falling tear;
And Leonardo, too, hath wept o'er Lucia's
  dusky pall,
And shrinks to hear the cold, dank clods upon
  her coffin fall;

The silent grave hath o'er her closed. She
    sleeps death's fair pale bride—
As sweet a flower, as e'er hath bloomed, or e'er
    in June hath died.

II.

The long, soft summer days have come and
    gone,
And Evelyn's fair young face, no longer wan
And wet with grief, its wonted color wears,
And oft she smiles, as erst in earlier years.
Within the sound of Arno's dashing foam,
Where the rough waters of the river roam
Around the base of rugged Appennine,
'Twixt banks of jasmine and the eglantine,
A Tuscan villa rears its sunlit dome—
'Tis Leonardo Vecchi's summer home.
Within its walls hath Evelyn's father found
Relief from care, and oft those halls resound
With Albert's chorus mingling with the strains
Of Evelyn's music, as the evening wanes;
And sometimes when the air is softly calm,
This youthful pair is rambling in the balm
Of eventide, to watch the eddying flow
Of Arno wandering on its way below;
Or slowly strolling thro' some sylvan vale,
When fire-flies twinkle in the twilight pale,
They list the warblings of the nightingale.

  'Twas thus the summer and the autumn
    passed,

And winter with its rude Trans-Alpine blast,
Around "fair Florence," too benign to roar,
Grows milder as he nears the Tuscan shore.
And now, in orange groves the orioles sing
Their grateful pœans to returning Spring.
Around the oak more closely clings the vine,
And tender hearts more closely yet entwine,
While blossoms catch the kisses of the dew,
And maidens meditate, and lovers woo.
'Tis twilight's quickening time, the trysting
    hour
Of orient climes, when trembling leaf and
    flower
Are shimmering in the star-light's silver sheen,
And silence softens all the sleeping scene.

Against the gothic gate, held half ajar,
Sweet Evelyn leans, more brilliant than the
    star
Her eyes have sought. With crimson lips
    apart,
Her life-blood bounding through her heart,
She lists to wooing words, which welcome steal
Within her yielding soul—love's first appeal.
What wonder was there Albert should adore
This young and lovely girl; that he should pour
His wealth of love on one so good and fair,
And warmly breathe it in her willing ear?

Like faint-remembered parts of some soft
    dream,
Young Albert's fervent tones to Evelyn seem;

As some sweet thought, the more 'tis pondered
    o'er,
The mind admits as once conceived before,
So dormant love, within her spirit stirred,
Enkindles newly with each whispered word.
These vows and burning words, in Evelyn's
    breast
Have warmed to flame a fervor unconfessed—
Love's latent sparks—its half-awakened gleams
Her heart hath harbored but in flitting dreams;
And yet, alas! these throbbings must be
    hushed—
Her love requited—by denial crushed!

   The fiat of her father's iron will
Hath quivered in her soul with sudden thrill;
Before her memory stands, iconoclast,
A startling spectre of the buried past—
Her hand betrothed e'en ere to girlhood grown,
That hand, by Albert asked, is not her own.
'Tis this she murmurs in her lover's ear—
By kind unkindness dooms him to despair.

   With sinking heart, another's promised bride,
Hath sorrowing Evelyn shrunk from Albert's
    side.
O'er Evelyn's tingling cheek and Albert's woe,
Come night, kind night, thy veiling vesture
    throw.

   Time's deep and hollow tones from yonder
    tower
Hath tolled the midnight's melancholy hour;

The rolling river, with its ceaseless moan,
Makes lone, sad hearts feel sadder and more
    lone,
Whilst Evelyn struggles with a vain regret,
Her sleepless pillow with her weeping wet.
And other eyes there are which cannot sleep,
Aye, other eyes that would but cannot weep:
Whole years of thought, of sober, solemn
    thought,
And high resolves that teeming brain hath
    wrought
Thro' that long night, and ere the early dawn
A rider leaves the gate. 'Tis Albert gone!

Gone, ay, gone—but he knows not, cares not
    where!
Ay, gone for many a lone and weary year!
Gone from the mellow meads and Tuscan vales,
Gone from the soft songs of the nightingales,
Gone from the citron-groves, where side by
    side,
He walked with his love in the eventide!
Gone with a load of grief upon his breast,
Anywhere, anywhere to find him rest!
    *   *   *   *   *
'Tis night—an Indian-summer's softest night;
  'Tis late, and the great city seems to sleep;
  The pale stars only their long vigils keep,
Mellowing harsh angles with their silver light;
  The city rests, and motionless lies all,
    Save in one quarter, thro' the lighted doors
And curtained windows of a princely hall
  A flood of merriment and music pours.

Within is Northern fashion's rich display,
   For Philadelphia's fairest of her fair,
Her wealth and pride, her gallant and her gay
   With sober age and jocund youth are there.
The hours to gladness and the dance belong,
To wine and wit, to sentiment and song;
Here matrons prim with gray-haired sires con-
     verse;
There moneyed merchants talk of Stock and
     Burse;
See, shyness shocked, is whispering of the faults
Of belles, less prudish, whirling in the waltz,
While timid girlhood, with her furtive glance,
Regards the bashful boy who claims the dance.

But follow we that form in spotless white—
Yon flitting form, so fairy-like and light.
See! how she walks the newly waxen floor,
As now she passes through the spacious door.
Beyond the bustling ball-room's showy glare,
To breathe the moisture of the morning air,
With memory busy at her bosom's core,
She seeks the quiet of the corridor!

Alas! the heavy heart may wear awhile,
Before the careless world its gayest smile,
E'en mirth may sparkle in the tear-wet eye,
Like sunshine thro' the showery April sky,
But soon that clouded heart, surcharged with
     grief,
Must break, or else in weeping, find relief.

That fair, familiar face is once more wan,

That winning smile she lately wore is gone;
Her tapering fingers to her young heart pressed,
The starlight stealing o'er her snowy breast,
Her pale, pale lips apart, she breathes a prayer,
Whilst in her eye there starts a trembling tear.
But scarce upon her lips that prayer hath died,
When stealing, like a spectre, to her side,
That kinsman, whom her inmost spirit loathed,
Her slighted suitor, scorned—her feared be-
    trothed,
Whom from her shrinking side, erst-while she
    spurned—
Her evil-genius hath again returned,
And there, beneath the dusky night's noon-tide
Hath clasped and claimed her as his promised
    bride.

"Ah, yes!" he whispers low, with flushing
    brow,
"Ah, yes! proud Evelyn, thou may'st scorn me
    now,
But by thy father's pledged and solemn vow,
By every word these lips have ever spoke,
By Richard Raynor's oath, which ne'er was
    broke,
And by our kindred blood I tell thee here,
Come weal, come woe, by foul means, or by fair,
That spurn me as you will, this hand of thine—
That heart—thy haughty self shall yet be
    mine."

His grasp is loosed; then speaks her woman's
    heart:

"Now hear me, Richard Raynor, ere we part!
By Him who rules our hearts—our God above—
By Him who knits together hearts in love,
By that unseen—that lithe, mysterious chain,
By which are linked in one the wedded twain,
By all the virtues which the soul adorn,
I tell thee, sir, this breast recoils with scorn
From hollow nuptial vows unblessed above,
From empty oaths that give the lie to love."

    *   *   *   *   *

    The restless wheels of Time are rolling on,
Year after year on gloomy wing hath gone;
Again Glen Arvon's garnished walls repeat
The sound of Evelyn's lightly falling feet.
Sole mistress of that mansion she presides,
By all beloved, and oft she gently guides
Her aged father to his cushioned chair,
Then steals away to hide the anxious tear,
That will unbidden start from eyes, as sweet
As ever father's fondest gaze did meet.
And sometimes, too, those love-lit eyes are dim
With tears, and yet those tears are not for him,
But nightly, as she lowly kneels to pray,
She weeps and prays for one who's far away—
Aye, far away, alas! she knows not where,
She only feels, to her how deeply dear,
'Neath Arctic skies, or Bengal's burning sun,
Is now the welfare of that absent one.
And often, too, he's flitting thro' her dreams,
As once he was, or else he lifeless seems,
A lonely corse, with glazed and ghastly eye,
Forever gazing on the glaring sky.

And thus, passed Evelyn's girlhood sadly by.
Meanwhile, those fearful years are drawing
 nigh,
Which soon must shake her country from its
 base,
And sweep, like simoom o'er her haughty race.
E'en now, those wrathful clouds are lowering
 nigh,
Which, tinged with blood, bedim the nation's
 sky—
E'en now, the muttering of the storm is heard,
From realm to realm the peaceful land is stirred,
Whilst freedom, turning pale with sad affright,
Hath plumed her wings prelusive to her flight!
That noble fabric by our fathers reared,
By blood cemented, and by all revered,
Alas! is tottering now, for discord there
Hath dwelt with angry look, for many a year.
Imperious power, despotic in its might,
Enthrones itself, defiant of the right.
It sends its minions thro' the startled land
In mad career, with naked steel in hand,
Till justice yielding all that she can yield,
Unsheathes her sword, and buckles on her
 shield!

III.

The moon looks down on Eutaw's classic
 plain,
Where sleep the ashes of the silent slain,
Where four-score years of winter winds and
 rains

Have scarce effaced the stubborn conflict's
    stains.
Beside the sunken graves of hero-sires,
Unflinching sons have lit their signal fires,
Which call the young and old from home and
    hearth,
And check the maidens in their Christmas
    mirth,
While weeping wives lament their parting ones,
And mothers mourn o'er battle-summoned sons.
'Tis Carolina pleads—they cannot pause—
Their lives are linked in one great, common
    cause,
'Tis Carolina calls, or right, or wrong,
To her their fortunes and themselves belong:
Few words they speak; in councils bold, but
    brief,
They gather round their gallant chosen chief;
Beneath yon flag, that flaps the frosty air,
'Tis Albert Ashleigh's voice breaks silence
    there:

"Sons of the South," he cries, "awake!
    To arms!   'Tis your country's call!
She bids you battle for her sake,
    Or with her freedom fall:
Forth to the field go meet the foe,
Defend her with your best blood's flow:
    To arms!   Give blow for blow
      For home and State!

"The Lord of justice knows your wrongs,
    He will be your strength and shield;

Only to craven slaves belongs
　The spirit that could yield:
Think of your country's honored dead—
Marion's brave men o'er Eutaw led—
　Remember how they bled
　　For home and State!

"Men of the South, awake! Arise!
　There is a victory to be won:
The glorious work before you lies,
　The battle is begun;
Up with the Lone Star! On ye brave!
Let its proud folds in triumph wave,
　To arms, if ye would save
　　Your home and State!

"Lo! the proud flash of beauty's eye
　Trusts her country to your care!
She bids you to the battle hie;
　Go with her holy prayer:
On, while a hostile soul survives!
On, for your sisters and your wives!
　Even your very lives
　　For home and State!

"Men of the South! What wait ye for?
　Your enemy is in the field;
'Irrepressible' is the war—
　Ye must not—cannot yield:
Must Southern men their wrongs be taught?
Can men, born free, so base be brought?
　Fight—as your fathers fought
　　For home and State!

"Men of the patient South, arise!
To your native land's release!
Be deaf to cries of 'Compromise'—
To coward calls for 'Peace':
Now is the day; no longer wait,
She bids you now decide her fate;
Arm! ere it be too late,
For home and State!"

Thus Albert speaks. A hundred youthful
braves,
Above whose heads the "Lone Star" banner
waves,
Beside him kneel on Eutaw's classic sod,
And there commit their country's cause to
God—
Beneath the stars of that cold Christmas sky
They swear for home and State to do—or die.

Ah! many a tear, that widowed hearts have
wept,
Attests how well that sacred vow is kept:
From solemn Sumter's sea-girt, shaken rock
To furious Antietam's desperate shock;
On many a bloody charge by Albert led;
On many a gory field they leave their dead,
Till few of all this patriot band remain—
The living few, who mourn the many slain.

* * * * *

Again 'tis night—a moonless, dark Decem-
ber night;
Strange sounds are heard from Stafford's can-

non-crested height—
Mysterious sounds, commingling with the mur-
    muring flow
Of Rappahannock, rushing o'er its rocks below:
All night the whispered bidding, and the muf-
    fled oar
Have reached the ear on Spottsylvania's
    guarded shore,
Where lie in wait those veteran heroes undis-
    mayed,
The iron-hearted Barksdale, and his brave
    brigade.
Three times their Northern foes have sought
    the Southern bluff;
Three times their bridge of boats has spanned
    the waters rough,
Before the Mississippians' deadly rifle fire;
Three times their reeling ranks with bleeding
    steps retire:
Full fifteen hours, with crashing shot and
    shrieking shell,
They storm the cliff—at length, with one heart-
    thrilling yell
Those stubborn men have crossed the troubled
    stream,
And o'er the quaking hills their bristling bay-
    onets gleam.
Now all the vales are torn by galling cannonade;
God help that small heroic band—that bold
    brigade,
Which will not turn and flee, but foot, by foot
    defends

The streets of Fredericksburg, for which the
    foe contends,
Till night again hath gathered o'er those top-
    pling spires,
Which front, like giant forms, the foemen's
    myriad fires.

    The long night wanes.   The pickets, on their
    silent posts,
Keep cautious, constant watch o'er Burnside's
    slumbering hosts.
Sleep on—for ere the morrow evening's star
    shall rise,
Full many a one in death's last sleep will close
    his eyes!

    Long rolls the loud reveille drum.   The army
    wakes.
O'er Fredericksburg's deserted streets the
    morning breaks,
While 'gainst the sky the "Southern Cross" is
    seen to shine—
'Tis lion-hearted Lee in long drawn battle line.
Lo! war-worn Longstreet's veteran corps, in
    grim array, ·
In patient, sullen silence, waiting for the fray!
See! yonder comes the young, but wondrous
    cannoneer,
Prompt Pelham, glancing o'er his guns with
    prudent care;
And Stuart, too, the dauntless, dashing cavalier,
The noble scion of a knightly race is there;

His falcon-eye hath spied fierce Sumner's
  chosen corps,
In double-quick time charging 'cross the hazy
  moor;
Then rings his clarion voice: "Up, gunners,
  to your posts!
Aim well, my gallant men! Hurl back the
  hireling hosts!"
One mingled burst of smoke; one long, low-
  rumbling sound—
War's iron messengers, with ricocheting bound,
Have smote the staggered foe, and in one common mound,
The dying and the dead bestrew the frozen
  ground.
A moment—and their rallying ranks have
  closed again:
With loud defiant shout they shake the trem-
  bling plain;
A hundred answering cannon, in their ruthless
  ire,
O'er hill and vale are belching forth their
  vengeful fire.

But who is he that furious, frenzied foe must
  front—
Whose bulwark breast must bravely bear the
  battle's brunt?
Behold him there, with lofty look, almost
  divine,
Fleet as the lightning, lead his legions into
  line!

As sweeps the swift Sirocco o'er the Lybian
main,
And leaves within its track a wrecked and
ruined train;
Now here, now there, with thunder force, above,
below,
He hurls his conquering columns 'gainst the
charging foe.
Ah! woe betide the rash assailants, who essay
To cope on battle-field with Jackson's giant
sway—
Resistless Jackson—besom of the bloody fray!

Meantime, not all the numbers of those
Northern hosts,
Not all the pristine prowess, which their coun-
try boasts,
Can reach that wall before Marye's embattled
height,
Where Kershaw and McLaws, unflinching, face
the fight.
Now, marching o'er the plain, in dashing mar-
tial style,
See Meagher's undaunted men of Erin's distant
isle—
Fierce scions of that fiery race, which won at
Waterloo
And Fontenoy's field of blood, come bursting
into view!

Their starry banners waving high,
Their bayonets gleaming 'gainst the sky,
The armies of the South defy—

Her chosen chivalry:
Forward they come with fife and drum,
Thro' sun and shade, 'neath cannonade
    And musketry!

The smoke, in columns, laps the plain,
The din that swells above the main,
Is echoed o'er the hills again
    In dreadful harmony!
'Neath shot and shell, with shout and yell,
They cross the glade and esplanade,
    Aye, gallantly!

On, on they come! Too late to pause,
They dash against the grim McLaws,
Onward, into the very jaws
    Of death, unflinchingly!
Their muskets flash, their bayonets clash!
O'er mangled dead the living tread
    Unsteadily!

As when rough billows, breaking o'er
The reefs of Hatteras' boisterous shore,
Turn, ebbing to the sea once more,
    Receding rapidly,
So backward borne, with banners torn,
Across the glen, these maddened men
    Press franticly!

Now sinks the blood-red setting sun;
Hushed is the hot, yet smoking gun;
The strife is o'er; the South has won
    That dear-bought victory.

That gory field the foemen yield,
Their bravest quail, whilst pennons trail
　　Despairingly!

The blushing moon is peering thro' the clouds
　　o'erhead,
Illuming all the grisly field of ghastly dead:
In doleful requiem, the night-wind's fitful
　　moans,
Anon, are mingling with the parting spirits'
　　groans.
See, o'er yon well-known form a group of sol-
　　diers sob—
'Tis Longstreet's fearless chieftain—Georgia's
　　gallant Cobb!
Sleep on, thou martyred hero, in thy glory
　　sleep!
Long o'er thy gory grave shall Georgia's chil-
　　dren weep,
And grateful for thy many deeds, the memory
　　keep
Of Cobb and victory.　Lo! there, a bleeding one,
That grand old leader, Gregg, the Southland's
　　promptest son,
Who fought for home and state, and scorned
　　the world's applause,
The first to draw his sword in Southern free-
　　dom's cause:
His lips, tho' pale and parched, in accents faint
　　and slow,
Are whispering words of cheer, with life blood
　　ebbing low:—
"Let Carolinians know, how cheerfully I die,

Contending for their rights—their homes and
    liberty.''
There, all but lifeless lies, on yonder litter
    borne,
A loved, but humbler one, whom faithful com-
    rades mourn;
With tearful eyes and swelling breasts they
    bear him on,
O'er field and tangled fen, and up the open
    lawn,
Within Glen Arvon's friendly door, where ten-
    der hands
Await to welcome wounded ones. There Eve-
    lyn stands!
They lay him at her feet, their blankets o'er
    him spread,
They leave him lying there, his knapsack 'neath
    his head.
That form they followed oft along the marches'
    toil,
Which led them o'er Manassas' twice victorious
    soil;
That cheering voice, which bade them ''charge''
    at Malvern Hill—
That form seems scarcely breathing now—that
    voice is still:
His brave young breast, so cruel torn by foe-
    man's shot,
Still true to Evelyn beats—yet Evelyn knows
    him not,
But patient, lingers there, to watch his waver-
    ing pulse,

While pangs of racking pain his fevered frame
    convulse.

   The anxious night hath passed, whilst Eve-
    lyn's careful hands
Have smoothed the choicest couch her father's
    home commands.
The winter's sun creeps slowly up the vaulted
    skies;
But once has Albert Ashleigh oped his languid
    eyes,
Then gazing into Evelyn's face with sweet sur-
    prise,
He breathes her name. "Oh! God," she cries,
    "it cannot be,
That Thou, my Lord, hast sent my Albert back
    to me!"
Again he faintly calls her name, yet still he
    sleeps,
Whilst Evelyn o'er his couch her faithful vigil
    keeps—
She kneels in prayer, then prints a kiss upon
    his brow,
And smiles between her tears, because she
    knows him now!

   Oh! ye, who in the midst of battle's fiercest
    storms,
Have weary, watched and prayed o'er loved
    and bleeding forms—
Ye widowed, weeping Rachels, whose heroic
    worth,

In secret, brightly shone beside the lonely
    hearth,
Who've felt war's whelming waters o'er you
    coldly roll—
Ye know what waves of anguish surged o'er
    Evelyn's soul!

IV.

The winter has vanished; the roses of spring
    Are kissed by the sun of the second of May;
The birds in the woodlands bewitchingly sing
    To hearts at Glen Arvon, that are happy
    to-day.

The daffodils bend 'neath the dew of the dawn,
    And pink-eyed anemonies enamel the way,
Whilst tiny wild daisies look up from the
    lawn
    At Evelyn and Albert, who are walking
    to-day.

Adown the gray rocks the rills ripple and
    bound,
    Far over the meadows in rhythm and play,
With many a mystical, musical sound,
    To welcome the loved and the loving to-day.

Yon roguish young robin, in flashing red vest,
    His throat all aglow with the joy of his lay,
Is chirping and chatting to his mate in her
    nest,

Of some one he knows, who is wooing
to-day.

The lark is aloft! See, how swiftly she flies!
But why is her song so enchantingly gay?
She laves her light wing in the blue of the
skies,
And warbles of one, who is happy to-day.

Adown the arched West sink the beams of
the sun,
Serenely the moments are passing away;
Two hearts at the mansion are beating as
one—
Two hearts at Glen Arvon are happy to-
day.

The evening wanes. Before Glen Arvon's
gate
There halts a courier, who hath ridden late,
And hurried leaves a note in Albert's hand—
A hasty summons to his new command.
No time for words; with one warm, fond adieu,
Hath Albert crossed the fields from Evelyn's
view,
Nor turns, nor reins his onward quick career,
Till warlike sounds have smote his soldier ear.

Once more, before Marye's embattled height,
Three thousand score of men, at dead of night,
In silent line, in battle's bold array,
Are anxious watching for the coming day.
Just as the first red streaks of early dawn

Have lit with life the Sabbath's sacred morn,
The foe, in phalanx strong, is scaling fast
Marye's rough ramparts to the trumpets' blast.
There Barksdale and his gallant band, again
Must meet the shock of twenty thousand men;
They fight, as never heroes fought before;
They fight till running rills of human gore
Have drenched the hills, yet still they stubborn
 stand
Before the foe, with muskets clubbed in hand.
Then 'gainst them Sedgwick bursts—his col-
 umns massed—
With force of avalanche, his corps at last,
On right and left, has turned their feeble flanks,
And backward bears their brave, unbroken
 ranks.
Still Barksdale bays the foe; he will not flinch,
But fighting yields the field, now inch by inch.

Oh! for the daring dash of Jackson now!
But woeful Sabbath morn! O'er Jackson's
 brow,
Alas! the dews of death are gathering fast,
While all the Southland, weeping, stands aghast!

Behold! meanwhile from Sedgwick's shout-
 ing corps
A rampant rabble sweeping 'cross the moor!
O'er field, o'er fence they bound; thro' brake
 and brush,
In reckless, wild career they onward rush,
And trampling o'er Glen Arvon's peaceful
 grounds,

They fiercely yell, till all the vale resounds.
But lo!· the leader of that lawless crew—
Yon form which stains with shame the North-
 ern blue!
Does trembling Evelyn mark that ruffian face—
The ruthless robber of her ruined race?
Too well, alas! that gloating eye she knows—
Most dastard of her country's dreaded foes!
Alas, that Richard Raynor's traitor hand
Should wield his sword against his mother-land!
Behold him rudely pushing thro' that door,
Which oft has kindly welcomed him of yore!
He strides across the hall to Evelyn's side,
And hails her roughly as his "rebel-bride."
"Come Evelyn, come," he cries—"my love—
 my life—
My pretty prisoner, now—ere long, my wife."

 "Thy wife, sir?" Evelyn asks, "I own with
 shame,
That Richard Raynor bears my worthy name;
I blush, that kindred drops course thro' our
 veins;
These tingling cheeks confess, dishonor stains
The bright escutcheon of our noble race,
But thine the deeds that doom it to disgrace:
Call me not 'wife!' With all thy subtlest hate ·
Strike at this heart! I'd bless thee for my fate,
Ere I would wed thee—traitor to thy state!"

 "Preach not to me," he tauntingly replies,
"More specious are thy rebel creeds than wise;
Go, call thy father, girl! for him I seek."

"There comes my father, sir, but far too
  weak
To bear the cruel words, methinks thou'lt
  speak."

"Well, sir! how fares it with mine uncle now ?
It seems, since last I saw that haughty brow,
Full many a trace of care hath o'er it crossed,
And war's rough years have added to the frost
Of winter on those locks.   But come! 'tis late!
To business now; yon chaplain at the gate
And these, my soldiers here, my bidding wait."

"Thy business, sir ? the old man asks, "Speak
  on:
What tho' thou be my dear, loved sister's son,
I hate the deeds thy father's race hath done!
Ye, one and all—our brethren but in name,
From pulpit and from press our land defame;
With   foul-tongued   clamor   and   maligning
  mouth,
Ye carp and cavil at the hated South:
Ye prate of peace, and yet, in savage ire
Ye desolate our shores with war and fire—
With chains and swords o'errun our fertile
  plains—
Swords for the valiant—for the vanquished,
  chains!
Your flag so honored once, on land and sea,
So long the symbol of a people free—
That flag which rallied erst the nation's braves,
No longer o'er their gallant lineage waves,
But license lends to mercenary knaves,

To bind us 'neath its folds as vanquished slaves,
Or fill our smiling South with bloody graves!
With earnest pride I, too, long, long upheld
That banner once, and oft this heart hath
    swelled,
Remembering all my perils, and the scars
Received beneath its conquering stripes and
    stars;
But long I've marked Virginia's bitter woe—
Myself have felt each fratricidal blow,
Which makes my country's rich, best blood to
    flow,
And ne'er again can call that flag my own,
Which costs Virginia one complaining groan."

That voice is hushed. With anger scarce
    controlled,
The other quick replies: "Thy words are bold—
Too bold for one, whose loud disloyal tongue
Would best be silent; for thou'lt find ere long,
Thy safety and thine Evelyn's, too, depends
On whom, as foes, thy rebel speech offends."

"Say on. What more does tyranny demand?
Would'st drive me helpless from my house and
    land?
If blood thou seek'st, thy minions I defy;
Thy grand-sire's son wilt teach thee how to
    die."

"Ye are my prisoners—thou and Evelyn,
    both:
I claim fulfilment of thy plighted troth—

Thy daughter's hand—renewal of thine oath
Of true allegiance to our nation's laws,
And firm resistance to this rebel-cause.
Refuse—and naught will save thee from the
    doom
Deserved, for yonder torches shall consume
These loved, these venerable ancestral halls,
Till not a stone of all Glen Arvon's walls
Shall one upon another rest—till all
It boasts shall in one common ruin fall.''

"Then hear me, Richard Raynor," he replies
Thine oath: thy high behests I all despise;
So, bid your heroes to their valiant work—
Fit deed for hand of Vandal, or of Turk!
For tyrant! I would see my daughter dead
By mine own act, ere I would have her wed
The traitor hand to which that sword belongs—
Foul, bloody symbol of her country's wrongs!
Would'st have me swear allegiance to that
    hand,
Which desolates mine unoffending land—
That hand which e'en its closest kindred
    smites—
Which ruthless robs me of my dearest rights?
Ye have spoiled me of my own—my all—'tis
    true!
Thank God! ye cannot touch my honor too!
Apply your torch! Bind on oppression's chains!
Thank God! at least, my honor yet remains!
Virginian born—Virginian I will die,
And meet my doom without one coward sigh!''

*   *   *   *   *

Beneath the dark shades of the gathering
gloom,
The flames of Glen Arvon the forests illume!
The flashes of blaze o'er the beeches arise,
The smoke, in black columns, envelopes the
skies;
Tall figures of foemen are gliding about,
Like demons of darkness, they dance and they
shout,
They revel and gloat, in their glee and their
hate—
Poor wretches! nor wot they their terrible fate!
A rider hath ridden, all reeking and hot,
Post haste to Glen Arvon, pursued to the spot:—
"Now, quick! to your ranks! to the river!" he
cries,
"The rebels are on us; a sudden surprise;
We are flanked; we are routed at Chancellors-
ville,
Where Jackson has fallen, but Stuart and Hill,
Revenging his fate, all their forces have massed,
And drive all before them as leaves on the blast,
Whilst Sedgwick defeated, is fast falling back
With Early and Wilcox like wolves on his
track!"

His warning comes late; ere its echo hath
died,
A troop of stout horsemen up gallantly ride—
Young Ashleigh their leader, as cavalier band
As sabre e'er drew in defence of their land!

Woe! woe to the foemen, who cower and flee,
Concealing themselves behind bramble and
 tree!
As falcons swoop down on each timorous bird,
The Southrons surround them—a panic-struck
 herd!
The captors are captive! But where is their
 chief
Hath wrought on Glen Arvon this ruin and
 grief?
What warrior so valiant—what soldier so bold
'Mong frail feeble women, the helpless and old,
As he, who alarmed, slinks away like the deer,
The first to scent danger, when battle is near!
But Albert is weary of carnage and death,
And orders his horsemen their sabres to sheath;
"No blood must be spilled! Men, remember!"
 he cries,
"For 'vengeance is Mine, saith the Lord' of the
 skies."

  *   *   *   *   *

Before Glen Arvon's ruined walls there stand
Brave Ashleigh and his Evelyn, hand in hand.
Ah! happy Evelyn, by her father blessed,
Her young head sheltered on his aged breast,
While 'neath the startled midnight's dewy air,
A chaplain weds the valiant to the fair!

  Weird wedding lights those waning midnight
 stars!
Strange witnesses those sturdy sons of Mars!
But Venus waits on bold Minerva's car,

And love must yield to sterner calls of war!

Off thro' the shadows of the night's noontide,
Beneath the solemn sombre trees they ride!
"God shield the soldier and his long loved
    bride!
God bless the old Virginian by their side!"
Off, off they go with blessings and with prayers
Of gallant Carolina cavaliers.

V.

Near two and twenty months of anxious
    hopes and fears,
Near two and twenty months of woman's
    yearning tears,
Near two and twenty mournful months have
    passed away,
Since that eventful, oft remembered night of
    May;
Whilst far from fearful scenes of battle and of
    blood,
Where close by Eutaw's plain steals Santee's
    sullen flood,
Beloved of friends, 'mid all that easy comfort
    gives,
In Albert's Carolina home his Evelyn lives—
Yet lonely lives, for sleeping 'neath the stran-
    gers' soil,
Her father rests, forever freed from war and
    toil,

And far away, on many a field's ensanguined
   marge,
Her own, courageous Albert leads the desperate
   charge.

Now war hath bared anew his blood-red,
   brawny arm;
Throughout the struggling South is heard the
   loud alarm!
The hydra-headed foe looms up from out the
   West,
And proudly lifts aloft his cruel, crimsoned
   crest;
His countless hosts rush down o'er Georgia's
   hapless soil;
Her fairest homes destroy, her temples all
   despoil.
What now avails the prowess of our valiant
   arms
'Gainst foes, which soon as fallen, rise in myriad
   swarms ?
Alas! our bootless sacrifice of bravest blood!
What arm of flesh can stay the whelming
   human flood ?
Now hourly sinking in the trembling scale of
   fate,
No hand, it seems, can save our shivering ship
   of state.
Our country's starry cross is seen to wave on
   high,
And ill-foreboding darkness dims the Southern
   sky.

Behold o'er Carolina's plains th' intruder
    sweep!
Behind him homesteads smoke! Lo, wretched
    women weep!
Behold the harrowing scenes of torture in his
    trail!
Hark, starving children cry! Alas, the woeful
    wail!

And now he nears the Santee's myrtle shaded
    shore;
O'er Eutaw's classic field his straggling minions
    pour:
Heaven help poor, trembling Evelyn in her
    lonely woe,
No loving, manly arm to shield her from the foe!
On, on they come! Weep, Evelyn, weep in
    blank despair!
The wolf his victim seeks; a worse than foe is
    near;
Thy nest he knows! Behold those eyes upon
    thee glare!
Behold the traitor, Richard Raynor, standing
    there!

Torn from her husband's home by force of
    vengeful foe,
As Richard Raynor's trembling prize compelled
    to go,
Now long and bitterly, poor Evelyn weeps.
    'Tis vain,
She goes, a guarded captive in the conqueror's
    train;

Beneath her kinsman's watchful eye, all woe-
begone,
She weeps till night, and thro' the dreary night
till dawn.
But ever on them both another human eye,
Tho' never seeming near, hath played the cau-
tious spy;
Familiar with each spot, it marks each path
and pass,
And deftly follows on the living, moving mass;
Yet never Evelyn recks, that Albert's faithful
slave
Against her captor plots, her wretched self to
save.

Another night is nigh—another night in
camp,
And Evelyn, shivering in the evening's pierc-
ing damp,
The foeman's fire hath sought. Her look of
blank despair
Gives way to wakened hope—that honest slave
draws near—
One cheering look of homage gives, then off
again,
He seeks the rebel camp of Hampton's gallant
men.
* * * * *
As gazes the eagle, with riveted eye,
Adown on his prey, from his eyry on high,
So Hampton, the chiefest of brave cavaliers,
Well worthy the chaplet of fame which he
wears,

Now watching the foe from his high bivouac,
Is rapt in regarding his point of attack.
Around him the night breezes fitfully sigh;
The cold moon above him is scaling the sky;
The spirit of Marion revives in his soul;
His country's lost hopes o'er him gloomily roll;
He reads in her strugglings poor Hungary's
     fate—
In Poland's dark doom the knell of his state.

    Below him is rolling the swift Edisto,
Beyond which carouses the confident foe,
The stragglers and revellers of Sherman's great
     hosts,
The negligent sentries, asleep on their posts,
Disgracing the camp of the conqueror's rear,
The rough and the rude, meet in rendezvous
     there.
And who so adapted this crew to command
As renegade Raynor, the scourge of his land,
Who, drunk with excesses of blood and de-
     bauch,
Uneasily tosses to-night on his couch,
Whilst Evelyn, poor captive, kneels down on
     the sod,
And tearfully lifts her sweet eyes to her God.

    Now Hampton descending—his eye on the
     foe—
Hath cautiously moved thro' the valley below;
His horsemen abreast on the river's rough
     slope,
Shall numbers so few with yon enemy cope?

No sinking of hearts at the difficult task—
'Tis Hampton who leads them—'tis all that
    they ask.
"My soldiers!" he tells them, "we cross not to-
    night
This turbulent stream a great battle to fight;
We need but a handful of cavaliers bold,
To rescue a prisoner yon revellers hold.
What tho' the wild flood at your feet swiftly
    sweeps,
'Tis innocence calling—a soldier's wife weeps
In yonder vile camp of the dissolute foe—
That soldier will lead you—my men, will ye
    go?"

"Aye, aye, we are ready!" cry all in a breath,
Aye, aye, lead us on!—to her rescue, or—
    death!"

As Albert, with hope beating high in his
    breast,
Selects from his comrades the bravest and best,
Behold a rude boat shooting out from the shore!
How stalwart the arm that is bending each oar!
How glowing that face—that dark face of the
    slave,
Exerting his strength the frail captive to save!
Twelve spirits, as buoyant as men on a hunt,
Now restless and reckless, have rushed to the
    front:
A dozen stout horsemen are swimming the tide;
They reach the dark bank of the furthermost
    side,

No more shall thy loved form be tenderly
    pressed:
Thine Albert is dead!   By his soldierly arm
No more shall thy Southland be shielded from
    harm:
His voyage down life's fitful river is o'er,
He reaches the realms of the limitless shore;
His spirit hath gone on the breath of the breeze,
To rest 'neath the shade of the Heavenly trees.

      *   *   *   *   *

In a mad-house doleful, dreary,
Evelyn wanders woful, weary,
In a mad-house lowly lying,
In a mad-house slowly dying—
    Slowly dying of despair:
With her soul forever saddened,
All her reason rambling, maddened:
Every night, a night of sorrow,
Hoping for the hopeless morrow
    Of a mad-house dark and drear!

Rests her Albert from his labor,
Sheathed beside him rusts his sabre,
Where the aspens pale and quiver
By the margin of the river,
    By the banks of Edisto.
But, thro' blissful, bright dominions
Soars his soul on spotless pinions,
Far beyond the shining river,
Waiting to be joined forever
    To that soul it loved below.